I0549818

Lady Justice

Children of the Goddess, Volume 3

Prudence MacLeod

Published by Prudence MacLeod, 2024.

Lady Justice

by

Prudence MacLeod

Book three in the Children of the Goddess series
Second edition.

LADY JUSTICE

First edition. January 13, 2024.

ISBN: 978-1927478479

Written by Prudence MacLeod.

Justice?

Tasha paced about her bedroom, fuming. Grounded? Sent to her room? She was twenty years old, for Christ's sake. She had taken part in a protest march, not a riot. She yanked the elastic from her long dark hair in frustration. Dammit anyway, this was wrong, so wrong. "I marched for justice, but there's no justice for me."

With a deep sigh she stepped before the mirror and took in her exotic looks. Her mom was first nations, and her dad was black. She had the long straight hair, high cheekbones, and lighter colouring of her mother plus the flashing eyes and dazzling smile of her father. That smile was nowhere to be seen this night.

Grounded, yeah, right. The hell she was. "I seriously need to get my own place." She swiftly dressed in black tights and tank top. A few essentials and spare undies in her backpack and she was ready to go. Tasha was just climbing out her window when she heard the front door crash inward. Loud shouts of "Get on the floor, Nigger. Now!" There were more shouts, her mother's scream, and then the gunfire.

Shocked, horrified, and trembling, she stood frozen, her stomach heaving, and listening to the voices from the main floor. "God damn it, Murdock, what the hell is wrong with you? Now we have to cover this up and hope like hell it doesn't cause another riot."

"He tried to kill me; you saw it Jim."

"I didn't see a damn thing, Murdock. He was unarmed and so was the woman. All right, boys, it's a goddam mess now. Search the rest of the house, find that damn kid and shoot to kill. No point making this any worse than it is. Damn niggers anyway. And make sure you get that cell phone."

At that command Tasha came back to life. All those years of gymnastics in school proved useful as she climbed out the window and swung up onto the roof. It was none too soon.

She heard the boots on her bedroom floor then the voice. "Ah crap, she was here, but she got out through the window. Probably three blocks away and crying to the media by now. There'll be hell to pay for this one. Shit. All right, let's get back to the station and get our story straight."

Trembling in fear, Tasha Stewart clung to the gently sloped roof, tears streaming down her face. It was over an hour later the ambulance and coroner arrived, but by then she had reached the ground and was gone. As the sun rose over the horizon, she broke down and sobbed her heart out in the basement of an abandoned building. "I didn't even go in to say good-bye to them," she wailed.

It took most of the day, but she cried herself out. Hunger eventually drove her out onto the streets. It wasn't until she tried to pay for the sub sandwich that she realized she didn't have any money with her, and she dared not use a bank card. She'd have to go back to the house.

Half a block away she spotted it, an unmarked police car. The house was being watched; they were looking for her. It suddenly hit Tasha that she'd been the original target all along. Her parents had been killed because of her. God damn it all, she'd only gone to a protest rally. They weren't terrorists.

They'd be called that, though. She burst into tears again and fled back to the abandoned building. She spent the night shivering in fear and the cold. She cried herself into a fitful sleep.

Tasha awakened slowly, fear gnawing at her very soul. She was no longer alone in the cold damp basement. The small hairs on the back of her neck were standing up and a shiver crawled slowly up her spine. "Relax woman," sighed a soft feminine voice. "I'm not going to hurt you." The speaker was a small girl not much older than Tasha. She had blue spirals painted on her face and arms.

"Who are you? What do you want?"

"I'm called Lady Blue. My name is Kara. Your name is Tasha and you're in deep shit. I'm here to bring you an option you might not have thought of. Hungry?"

"What do you mean options? Wait, what? Yes, I'm starving. Have you got anything to eat?"

"Sure, try this." She tossed Tasha a couple of military ration bars then fished a bottle of water out of her backpack. She passed it over.

Tasha forgot everything in her hunger. She devoured the bars then guzzled the water. A moment later she became aware of the small girl watching her. "These are military rations, where did you get them?"

"I took them off a soldier who tried to rape me. Feeling better now?"

"Yes, I am, Thanks. Wait, what did you mean about options? What were you talking about? What do you know about me?"

"I know all about you, Tasha. I know what happened to you and your family. I wish I could stay and help, but I have another errand that can't wait." She began wiping the blue greasepaint off her face. "Here, take this and wipe your face; you've got mascara everywhere from crying." Tasha gratefully accepted the offered wipe and cleaned her face.

"Better?" Tasha nodded her thanks. "Tasha, I know what you're thinking of doing. Bad idea, girl."

"Wait. What? How do you know what I'm thinking? Are you psychic or something? Can you read minds?"

Kara smiled at that. "Nope. I know because Moragah told me. She told me everything. Moragah knows you want to kill those guys and she wants to talk to you about that."

"Who or what is Moragah?"

"Moragah is the goddess of wisdom, defender of the weak."

"A goddess. Right." Tasha rolled her eyes then shrieked as Kara leaped to her side.

"Relax, woman. Geez. I'm not going to hurt you. Take my hand."

Reluctantly, Tasha reached out and took the small hand in her own delicate fingers. Instantly she was aware of that vast presence surrounding her, comforting her, driving the pain and anguish from her mind. "Do not fear me, my child. I will not harm you, but yes, I do exist." There was warmth and humour in that voice that sounded in her mind and Tasha relaxed completely. "Listen to Kara; hear what she has to say with an open mind."

At that, Kara released Tasha's hand and the presence of Moragah withdrew from her awareness. She shivered as the cold and dampness of the old basement returned. "All right, now that we have that out of the way..."

"Okay, that was totally weird...but nice. I don't even care how you did it. So, what's the deal?"

"The deal is simple. You want to kill those guys who shot your family. I don't blame you for that; I would too. However, that'll just get you killed as well. Moragah wants something more for you. She wants to help you, and She wants you to help Her."

"Ah-huh. So, what does this magic goddess of yours want to help me do?"

"What you want to do; what you wanted to do before this happened. She tried to prevent that, but I got here too late."

"Too late for what?"

"To stop what happened to your family. I was halfway across the country when I got the call. I'm sorry, Tasha."

"Stop it? How could you have stopped it?"

"I have my ways," sighed Kara. "It's all changed now. At first I was supposed to stop the killing of your family then talk to you about your efforts to bring justice to the people of this city; your crazy desire to help people even though they don't want anything to do with you because you're not like them. Now it's all changed. Something else has come up and I have to move on."

Kara rose to her feet and reached for her backpack, but Tasha stopped her. "Wait, that voice said to talk to you..."

With a sigh, Kara sank back to a cross-legged position on the floor. "Okay, here's my story. I was twelve when I was kidnapped in front of my school. I was raped and forced into prostitution out on the west coast. A few years of horror later I was rescued by Lady Blue."

"Lady Blue, you said you are Lady Blue."

"One of. I was made a priestess of Moragah after the rescue. I couldn't fit back into a normal life, you see. Anyway, we call ourselves Lady Blue. I have no real idea why, but I think it has something to do with the sacred spirals we paint on our faces when we go to war with the bad guys. Moragah made me a priestess; that gave me a reason to stay alive. Now I kick ass, take names, and stay one step ahead of both the cops and the criminals I fight."

"Kick ass, right."

"Hey, I may be small, but I'm mighty," grinned Kara.

"Ah-huh."

Kara sighed and lowered her eyes to the floor. "I see a demonstration is in order."

Tasha shrieked as Kara exploded from the floor and blurred out of sight. She was moving too fast for the eye to follow. A support post was yanked from its station and the floor groaned above them as the post was shattered into splinters. Kara came back into view, breathing deeply. She glared at the wood, and it burst into flame. A moment later Kara reached out her hand and closed it into a fist; the flames died instantly.

She smiled at Tasha who sat pressed tightly to the wall, her hands covering her mouth. "That's just a sample. I can do other things too. For example, I always know what direction to go, I can hear at distance if I concentrate. You know, stuff like that."

"Oh my god," Tasha breathed softly.

"A priestess of Moragah has superpowers, we all do. Some are different. For example, Penny can run right up the side of a building. Man, she's awesome."

"How many of you are there?"

"As far as I know there are three of us now. Look, I have to go. Talk to Moragah before you do anything else, okay? Just talk to Her. If this life isn't for you there'll be no hard feelings." Kara swept up her backpack and jogged up the stairs.

"Wait. What???"

"Talk to Her, Tasha, just talk to Her. Don't do anything else until you talk to Moragah." With that, Kara disappeared through the door.

Tasha ran up the stairs, calling for her to wait. "Hold on a minute..." She stood gazing all around, up and down the street. There was no sign of Kara, the tiny wonder woman. "How the hell did she...? Oh well, that was all totally weird. Maybe I imagined it all.

"Doesn't matter. I need to go home. I need some cash, a shower, some of my clothes, and...oh god, Mom and Dad..." Fighting back the emotions that threatened to consume her, Tasha headed for what had once been her home.

The house was still being watched. Dammit anyway. Tasha faded back along the street and pulled out her phone. It was dead. Double damn. She knew she couldn't continue on the way she had been. She needed help so she headed towards her best friend's place.

That house was being watched too. What the hell? She circled around to the alley behind the house and whistled softly. On her third try she got a response. "Shhh, Tasha, is that you? Run, girl. The cops are everywhere looking for your head. Run."

She ran. Tasha had been back at her hideout for about an hour when she heard someone approach. "Tasha, you here?" called a soft voice.

"Denise, is that you?"

"No, I'm somebody else. Of course it's me. Who the hell else would it be? Don't look so disappointed. Who were you expecting, Wonder Woman?"

"I had hopes," sighed Tasha as she sank to the floor and rested her head in her hands. "Man, I am so screwed."

"You'll be worse than that if they catch you, girl." Denise sank to the floor beside her. "What did you do?"

"Nothing, I swear, Dennie. I went to that protest rally, but it was pretty peaceful. The cops threw their weight around, but nobody started anything. As usual they denied shooting that guy, the politicians promised to get to the bottom of it, and nothing at all will ever come of it. Same shit, different day.

"It started to break up, so I went home. When I got there, Mom and Dad were in a fit. They tried to ground me, for god's sake. Oh god, Mom and Dad..." She burst into tears again and Denise put her arms around the distraught girl. "Sorry," sniffed Tasha as she regained control of her emotions.

Denise released her then sighed. "The cops say you were on drugs, went nuts, and shot both your parents."

"Sure I did. Did they explain how I managed to have a loaded police special?"

"No," chuckled her friend. "They left that part out. Look, Tash, you gotta get out of town. Things have gone completely crazy around here now. You know those guys will shoot you on sight. Tash, I don't think the Association will help you either, you know..."

"You mean because I'm not black; I'm just a mutt?"

"Hey, you know Mr. Gimbal didn't really mean that. He was just upset and..."

"Let his true feelings slip?"

Denise hung her head and sighed. "Yeah, maybe. It's just fear talk, Tash, you know that. Everybody is so damn scared for their lives these days. Shit, if my dad even thought I was here talking to you..."

"He'd freak, right? It's okay. He just wants to keep his family safe. I get that. Man, I am so screwed. I don't have any money, I don't dare use a bank or credit card, and I stink. I need a shower, I need clean clothes, and I need to think. You go on home, Dennie. Be careful and I'll let you know where I end up if I survive."

Denise kissed her friend's cheek, hugged her tightly, and then rose to go. "Here's twenty bucks. It's all I have."

"Thanks, sweetie. I'll pay you back...someday."

"You'd better. Be careful and get out of town as quick as you can. I won't see you again for a while, Tash. Dad is sending me out of state to college."

With that, her only friend was gone. Tasha sank into a depression and cried herself to sleep. She dreamed. In her dream Kara, a taller blonde, and an Asian girl, all wearing blue tattoos, came and sat with their backs to her, guarding her rest.

Suddenly feeling safe, Tasha relaxed into a deeper sleep and the dream faded. She awakened several hours later, hungry but feeling rested. Refreshed.

Tasha went to the far corner and relieved herself then returned to the pile of crushed cardboard she'd slept on. It was time to make a plan. She couldn't go on the way she was, she had to do something, anything. Maybe she should talk to a lawyer. It was as good a plan as any.

Arrested

The constant tapping of her foot was driving the officer crazy. A part of Tasha Stewart was enjoying that. She wasn't enjoying the rest. She had chosen a lawyer at random. Reluctantly, he agreed to take her case. The first thing he did was convince her to turn herself in to the police. He went with her to make sure she was kept safe.

Now they sat in a small room with two officers, a man and a woman. It was quiet now. For several minutes the male officer had shouted at her, leaning across the desk aggressively. "Why did you kill your parents?"

Tasha's response was the same every time. She shrank away from the angry man and said, "I didn't, you did."

Finally, the female officer broke the silence. "Where's your cell phone, Tasha? You didn't have it with you."

"I guess I lost it when I ran."

"That's a goddam lie," roared the male officer. "Where's the damn phone?"

"I lost it," she shouted back, breaking at last.

"Can we speed this up?" asked the lawyer. "I have to be in court in twenty minutes."

"Fine, we're done here," growled the male officer. "Put her in a holding cell." He rose and stormed out of the room.

The lawyer followed as they put Tasha in a cell and the door clanged shut behind her. "I'll be back after court to get you out of here. Don't worry." As she walked away she heard him speak to the male officer. "I don't know where her phone is, she didn't have it with her when she came to my office."

"They seemed pretty friendly," she mused as she sat on the floor, drew up her knees, and buried her face in her arms. A couple of hours later the lawyer returned and she was released. That seemed odd to her. He offered to drive her to a shelter, but she refused and jogged down the street.

Certain she wasn't being followed, Tasha returned to her hideout. "I wonder what's on this that has them so messed up," she mused as she retrieved her phone from its hiding place.

"Freeze right there," barked a loud voice.

Tasha panicked and ran. She dodged behind an old furnace and tried to wriggle out a broken window. She made it and got to her feet but was instantly tackled to the ground. She fought as hard as she could, but it was useless. Slowly a voice penetrated her panic.

"Stop it. Hold still girl. They want to kill you; I'm trying to keep you alive. Hold still. Don't fight me. Don't give them an excuse. Be still now." It was the female officer that had been in the interrogation room. "It's all right. I've got her."

"Listen girl, don't say a word, don't make eye contact, and don't try to run. I'm going to secure you now, be still and I'll keep you alive." Tasha was vaguely aware that the woman was keeping her own body between her prisoner and the officer rushing into the alleyway.

"Move aside, I'll cover her."

"Put your damn gun away, Martin. She's in restraints and there's no fierce poodles here for you to shoot."

"Fuck you, Jess."

"Not in this lifetime you won't," growled the woman as she gently helped Tasha to her feet. She guided the girl into the back seat then turned to her partner. She flinched at the sound of the gunshot. "What the hell was that?"

"Her cell phone," grinned the overweight policeman. "She tried to run; I fired one shot, missed her and hit the cell phone. It's not much good for evidence now."

Shaking her head, the female officer got into the car. Her partner climbed behind the wheel and started the car. "You planning to bunk with her tonight, Jess?" he asked.

"What is that supposed to mean?"

"As soon as we go off shift they'll get to her, you know that. She won't last the night."

"Then I'll spend the night." Tasha heard the conviction in the woman's voice and was somewhat reassured. Alas, it wasn't meant to be. As soon as Tasha was in a cell Jessica Logan settled down at her desk.

"Working late, Logan?"

"Yeah, I've got some paperwork to catch up on, Sarge."

"It'll keep. Go home."

"Nope, I gotta get this done."

"I said go home, Logan. That wasn't a suggestion."

"Are you making that an official order?"

"If I have to."

"You do."

"Then it's an order. Your shift is finished. Go home."

"Fine. I'll just check in with my prisoner. Make sure she's all right before I go."

"Why the hell would you care? It's just another half nigger kid gone crazy on drugs."

"Let's say I take my job seriously, unlike some people around this station."

He snorted derisively and walked away. However, he watched carefully as Jessica checked in with Tasha then reluctantly left the building.

A short while later Tasha overheard two of the men talking. "So, how we going to do this one, Sarge?"

"Same as always. Kid on drugs hangs herself in the cell. We'll tie her bra around her neck then string her up."

"Okay, let's get to it."

"Wait. It's early yet. We'll wait until closer to morning. It'll give the boys more time to search that hideout of hers. You know, just in case she made copies."

"Sure. Anything show up on the internet?"

"Nope, not yet."

"Thank God. We'll be able to keep a lid on this one after all."

"Yep, just one small loose end to tie off."

"Is Logan going to be a problem?"

"She'd better not be."

Both men laughed at that and walked out of her hearing range. Tasha was both terrified and horrified. That was when she remembered Kara and that goddess. That had all seemed so unreal. There was no other option now. She moved into the corner and sank to the floor hugging her knees. Silently, she began to pray.

"Great Moragah, please hear this prayer. Please help me. They're going to kill me; I know they are. Please hear me. Please help."

Instantly, Tasha felt that vast presence surround her, comforting her, easing the pain in her body from the restraints. "Be at peace, Tasha. I am with you. No harm will come to you while I am here. Tell me now, what do you want me to help you with?"

"Saving my life would be great for starters. They're going to kill me and say I committed suicide. They going to say it was because I shot my parents and couldn't live with myself."

"Is that all you want?"

"You could help me kill those bastards who killed Mom and Dad."

"Yes, I could do that."

"But why would you?" sighed Tasha. She began to sink into a depression. If the goddess wouldn't help she was already dead. There would be no justice for her parents, for her.

The voice of Moragah came again, gentle and loving as a new mother. Tasha felt comforted, hopeful. She began to relax from her fear. "The real question, Tasha, is, why would you?"

Tasha sat up straighter. "Why would I? They killed my parents, that's why."

"For vengeance?"

"Yes. I want to avenge them, them and everybody else those bastards have murdered or abused in the past few years."

"Everybody else?"

"Yes. All the black people, the first nations people, the Mexicans, the poor whites that hate us anyway, and all the other people who get used, abused, and killed by corrupt police every day."

"Tasha, there is a darkness falling over this country of yours. Vengeance will only feed the darkness. Evil brings more evil with it. What would your father say about your desire for vengeance?"

"He would say, 'Vengeance belongs to God, not to men.' So, what am I supposed to do? Run away and hide my head in the sand? Get lost and forget all about them and the bastards who killed them?"

"What do you truly want to do here? If I make this possible for you, what would you truly want to do?"

Tasha sat thinking for a moment. This was it, the final moment. She knew her answer would make the difference in whether Moragah would help her or not. "I guess if you could change everything about this world you would have done it already. For me, I think I want Justice. Not blind justice, but real justice for my parents, for the people. Real justice, real in your face right now justice, no lawyers and politicians messing it up and dragging it out, and no waiting generations for Karma to work it out. Justice that can't be bought out by the rich or scared off. Cold hard justice.

"So tell me, Moragah, what do you want? Kara said you sent her to me. Why? What do you want from me?"

"Justice, even as you do, my child. This darkness falling disturbs me. The cries of the innocent and the laughter of the oppressors, cause me great pain. I am deeply troubled."

"Can't you do something about it? Make it stop?"

"I have my limits, Tasha, even as you do. No, I can only directly affect the lives of humans by acting through other humans. So, I create my priestesses and help them as best I can. I have created three priestesses to defend the weak, to right the wrongs that they encounter. This they do well, and I'm quite proud of them.

"Tasha, when I create a priestess, I become a part of her, always with her, every moment of every day. Each morning she faces the rising sun and greets me, honouring my name. In return I bestow great power upon her. This is how it is. This is what I wanted for you too when I first sent Kara to you."

"But not now?"

"No, no longer. The three greet the sun each day and are children of the light. Sadly, they cannot hold back this darkness. We will not be able to stop it, but it's my hope we can give it pause, create a small light the darkness cannot extinguish. For this purpose I need a priestess of the shadows, of the night.

"She will be a woman of terrible power who greets me through the moon as darkness falls. She will still wear the sacred spiral to honour me in her task, but her tasks will be darker. Her task will not be to stop the bad things, that is for the others to do. No, this priestess will seek out the truth then deliver justice, a dark and swift justice.

"Yes, Tasha, this is what I want. I want you to be my shadow priestess. I want you to root out the evil, the oppressors, and deliver justice, at least for some of the fallen."

"You want me to right all wrongs everywhere?"

Moragah chuckled again. "No child, there will always be injustice in the world. I ask only that you deal with whatever crosses your path."

"Like my parents?"

"Yes, their case will be the first order of business."

"But I can't kill the bad guys."

"Of course you can, especially if they attack you or another innocent, just not in anger or vengeance."

"So, what if I provoke them a little..."

Again she felt Moragah's mirth and it made her smile. "That's a line both Penny and Kara walk all too often. In your case it won't matter. You will punish the guilty without conscience. You will have no need to wait for an attack. I only ask that you do not act in vengeance or anger."

"Okay, I get it, and I like it. Moragah, we're running out of time here. How does this work?"

"I choose abilities from your mind to enhance you with. I also enhance your natural abilities. For you I will also choose a purpose for I have seen the Punisher in your mind. Be warned, the process is extremely painful, but it lasts for only a heartbeat. Brace yourself."

Tasha nodded that she was ready. At least she thought she was ready. Suddenly every cell in her body burst into hellfire, ripping a soul searing scream of anguish from her lips. It was over in an instant, but it left her gasping for breath. Moragah enfolded her, filling her with feelings of well being, soothing her hurts until she was at peace again.

"Thank you Moragah. So, I have superpowers now?"

"You do."

"What are they?"

"Whenever you're threatened or in combat you will move at great speed. You now have the strength of ten men and more, that will be magnified by your speed. By focusing on people at distance you will be able to hear them speak. All your injuries will heal almost instantly. You will be able to hide yourself just by remaining still. Also, you will sense when danger threatens. There is more, but that is enough to begin with."

"They're coming for me now, aren't they?"

"Yes."

"Oh god, what am I going to do?"

"Do what you must, my child. I have prepared you. The task is yours now." With that, Moragah pulled back from Tasha's awareness.

Suddenly alone and terrified, Tasha fought her restraints. They parted instantly. It was easy as breaking a small child's grip. She waved her hands through the air for a moment, a smile of delight reaching her face. "Cool!" She jerked the shackles from her legs and leaped to the cell door. It was locked tightly. "Shit! Now what do I do? Okay, hide in plain sight, She said. Let me see if it works."

Pressing her back to the concrete wall, Tasha tried to quiet her mind. "I'm invisible, she breathed silently. "You can't see me. There's nobody here. This is not the cell you're looking for."

A man was whistling tunelessly as he approached the cells. Without looking closely, he unlocked her cell and swung the door wide. "All right, kid, this is going to hurt you more than it does me...What the fuck? She's gone!" he bellowed.

"What the hell do you mean, she's gone?" demanded another as he came running.

"I mean she's gone, as in the cell is empty, there's nobody home, no kid, empty cell. Which one of you morons let her loose?"

"What the hell? It had to be Logan. She must have..."

"Just walked into the station, took your keys, unlocked the cell, and spirited your prisoner away and you didn't see shit. Is that your story?"

"We don't have time for this crap," snarled another as he approached. "Get out there and find her. All of you get going!" The big man stood with his back to the cells, muttering to himself. "I knew damn well I should have waited until the bitch was in the room before I gave the nod to open fire. We could have gotten all three at once."

"Now that's good to know," came a soft voice behind him.

The big officer spun around to see his quarry. "Well, whaddya know, today's my lucky day."

"No it isn't," she snarled as he reached for her. He was thrown across the room where he slammed into the wall. Before he could recover, her arms encircled his head. He struggled weakly, but she was too strong. "My name isn't bitch, it's Justice. Justice has come for you, asshole; time for you to face the music." She gave a sharp twist, his neck snapped, and he sank lifeless to the floor as she released him.

"I just might have a use for these," she mused as she took his weapons belt and tossed it over her shoulder. She took the money from his wallet too. "Now, this is your donation to the justice fund, asshole." Still running on adrenalin, she bolted through the front doors and across the parking lot into the shadows. She had moved too swiftly, no one saw her pass.

The Search for Justice

Tasha ghosted along the sidewalk, stopping twice to wait for the searchers to pass her by. Finally, she felt she was in the clear. A small park provided cover for the new shadow priestess, and she sank to the ground in relief. "Oh god, that was scary."

"I know," came the voice of Moragah as the vast presence surrounded her again, soothing her, calming her. "You did well, my priestess. I am proud of you."

"Thank you, Moragah. I killed that policeman. I heard him say he gave the go ahead to shoot my parents."

"Yes, he has faced Justice for the many deaths he has caused."

"I took his gun and wallet. Does that make me a thief? A criminal?"

"It was just, my daughter. Because of him so much more was taken from you. Besides, you need to maintain yourself if you are to continue the quest successfully."

"I guess you're right. I need to eat, I need a shower and clean clothes, and then I need to sleep. What am I going to do?"

"What you must," replied Moragah, the mirth clear in her voice. "My child, trust yourself and your new abilities. You will use them instinctively if you relax and allow yourself to be. Don't try to over think things, just go with it as you did during the jailbreak."

"Like I did, wait, what? Oh, right. When I hid against the wall? Was that mind control?"

"Akin to it, but not quite. Call it a strong power of suggestion."

"That's another one of my abilities?"

18

"Indeed so." With that Moragah withdrew.

"Sure, fine." Tasha sighed. "Use my abilities, trust myself. Okay, maybe I should for a change. So, where to start? Food, shelter, and a shower. Where? How? Home, that's where I need to go. There'll be food and a shower, fresh clothes, and maybe other useful things." She rose easily to her feet and set out.

She hadn't gone far when she saw the police car. Melting into the shadow of a tree, she focused on the car. She could hear the voices clearly. "Cruiser thirty-six here, and clear. No sign of the perp anywhere."

"Roger that. Maybe the kid went home. Go check it out and keep an eye on the place."

"Copy that, thirty-six out." As the policeman hung the radio back in the cradle he saw a shadow out of the corner of his eye. He put the car back in park and squinted at the shadows. Something moved. Slowly, with gun drawn, he got out of the car and went for a closer look. "Nothing, just your damned imagination, moron," he muttered to himself as he put the gun away and returned to the car.

He was still grumbling as he got back in, then he noticed the girl sitting in the passenger's seat. Startled, he reached for his gun, but she grabbed his wrist in a vice-like grip. "Relax, Officer, relax. Just listen to my voice and relax." Not quite sure why he did, the officer relaxed.

"You're that kid. The one who killed her parents then killed the sarge at the precinct station."

"I did kill the sergeant, but I didn't kill my parents, Officer. You were ordered to go to my house and watch. We can talk while you drive. I want to go home, but it's a long walk. Go on now, drive me home."

He started the car and pulled out onto the street. "We both know it was the police who killed my parents," she said in that soft soothing voice. "Was it you?"

"No, I wasn't on shift that night." He replied as though he was in a trance.

"I heard them talking. The man who shot them was called Murdock. Do you know him?"

"Yes. It wasn't Murdock."

"Oh, why do you say that? Were you there?"

"No, I was off shift that night, but Murdock is a straight arrow. They've been trying to get rid of him for a while now."

"That's good to know. Do you know Officer Jessica Logan?"

"Yes, Logan is another straight arrow. Nobody trusts her."

"Oh, why not?"

"She won't back you. If it gets crazy and a bystander gets hurt, Logan won't back your story. She's not one of us, and neither is Murdock anymore. Well, here we are at your house."

"Very good, Officer. What are your orders?"

"I'm supposed to look for you at the house and if you're not there to watch the house in case you come back."

Her voice was so soothing, he unconsciously obeyed her every wish. He really wanted to please her, to make her like him. "Look closely at the house now, can you see me in there?"

"No."

"Good, now report in that you can't see me at the house. You don't believe I will come back here."

Obediently, he picked up the radio. "Unit thirty-six reporting in."

"Go ahead thirty-six."

"I'm at the perp's house. Can't see any signs of her there."

"Very good, Ciccone. Stay there and keep a sharp eye out."

"Roger that. Thirty-six out."

"That's perfect, Officer Ciccone. Sleep now, you need to rest through the night. Sleep and be at peace." Slowly his eyes closed. He folded his arms across the steering wheel and leaned his head on them. He was asleep and unaware as she got out of the car.

Her bedroom window was still open, so she returned to the inside by the same route she'd used to leave; up the tree and through the window as she had so many times before. This time the house felt cold, empty, and sad. Shaking off the mood she stripped off and headed for the shower. At least there was still hot water.

Tasha couldn't remember when a shower had felt so good. After she dried off and dressed in clean clothes she headed down to the kitchen. She stopped at the bottom of the stairs, her hand flying to her mouth. There were two chalk outlines on the floor, the carpet stained a deep red from the blood. This is where her mother and father had died trying to protect her.

Swallowing the lump in her throat, she stepped carefully around the outlines and went to the kitchen. Everything in the fridge was spoiled, but there were cans of food in the cupboards. She built a plate full, heated it in the microwave, then enjoyed her first full meal in days.

Tasha returned to her bedroom with a full belly. As tempted as she was to curl up in her own bed, she knew she dare not. She packed a few changes of underwear, spare leggings and a couple of tank tops in a small backpack. Dammit, the cops had her good backpack which would hold more. Ah well.

What else would she need? Her eye fell on her flute case and she sadly shook her head. There would be no way to carry that in the coming days. She scooped up her tin whistle, pulled on a dark hoodie, and went out through the window again.

The neighbours were still away on holiday. She crept into their yard and tested the windows of the house. Finding one unlocked, Tasha slipped inside. She slept through the night on their couch then left a note in the morning, thanking them for the hospitality. Next morning she caught a bus nearby and moved deeper into the inner city. She needed a new hideout.

Meanwhile, believing she would try to run, the police had all possible exits from the city covered. There was no way she could leave town, but then, she didn't really want to.

After three days of intensive searching, things quieted down. The police had no way of knowing the object of their search had gone to ground deep in the city's forgotten underground. A helpful homeless man had shown her a path through the sewers to an abandoned railway station with one railway car still intact. Justice had a new home.

A New Ally

Tasha took a slow careful look around in the flickering light. This place was part of an old subway line that had been abandoned. The room was quite large, and the single subway car was intact. Her candle guttered and nearly went out. "Hmmm, I'll need some battery-operated lights and a sleeping bag would make a passable bed, I guess. What else will I need?"

She sighed deeply and her shoulders sagged. "I'll need another way out of here is what I'll need. Okay, first I need a good flashlight and a sleeping bag. I'll need food too. Damn, living like this will sure make it easy to stay on the diet.

"The car is big enough to use as an office too. All I need is some equipment."

She sighed and sank to the floor of the old car as her candle went out. "Aw crap." Tasha prepared herself to feel her way towards the door and the exit hole beyond when she suddenly realized her vision was clearing. Her eyes were adjusting to the darkness. "Oh my god, I can see in the dark."

"Yes you can, my priestess."

"Lady Moragah, you're awesome."

"Thank you, Tasha. So, you have found a new home."

"Yes and no. I understand that I could have to abandon this place at the drop of a hat. I know I'll never have a home again, but this will do nicely as a base of operations. I need a place in the heart of the city that's completely hidden. If I was rich like Batman, it would be different, but I'm not. This is going to be hard."

"Oh, in what way?"

"Well, I'm supposed to be Justice, right? I can't just go steal the stuff I need, can I? If I'm going to get to the bottom of what happened and why I need a few things, tools, and I can't steal them, so I have to find another way."

"Moragah, how do the others manage it?"

"Well, at first Penny took what she needed from the bullies she encountered. Their evil made their possessions and resources fair game, as she would say. She later encountered people willing to help her, but she still forages from the bullies, the users and abusers. So do the others."

"So, they take what they need from the bad guys?"

"Yes, as well as from other sources. For example, you found a ride home and then a place to rest for the night. You brought no harm to anyone when you did."

"Okay, I can work with that. You said Penny found allies. Is that okay to do?"

"Yes, for this task you will need allies from time to time. Be wary of who you trust, but you will need allies."

"Yeah. I think I should talk to that policewoman, Jessica Logan. She was careful to protect me when they caught me, and she was pissed when they wouldn't let her stay to watch out for me that night. I also have to find that Murdock who shot my mom and dad. He's way up on my list."

"Are you certain he's guilty? That other policeman didn't seem to think he would do that."

"I remember. Don't worry, Moragah. I won't do anything until I'm completely convinced. Okay, first things first. I have to find where they buried Mom and Dad, and then I need to outfit this place. Since I can see in the dark, I might as well take a look around for an escape hatch before I do anything else."

"I shall leave you to it, my daughter." Moragah gave her another wave of sweet energy then pulled back to let her work. It took Tasha only moments to find the weak source of light that allowed her to see. It was a crack in the concrete that sealed off this section of the subway.

Sweeping up a huge stone she battered at the concrete. It fell away disclosing a steel access door. It was locked, but it was a poor fit and light was coming in around it. The extra light really lit up the place for her enhanced eyes. She battered the rusty handle and heard the lock shatter inside. A quick jerk opened the door. A train was rushing by.

Tasha stood on the narrow ledge waiting until the train passed. Once it was safe she jogged down the line. It turned and there was the platform. Grinning, she hopped up and made for the stairs leading to the street above. She was in a poor section of town. Everything was run down and neglected. It didn't take her long to find what she wanted.

The drugs and money changed hands before the three young men noticed her approaching.

"Wha choo lookin' at, Bitch? What's a hoe like you doin' here anyway?"

The dealer's day took a sudden bad turn. She grabbed him by the collar and threw him against the wall. "Don't call me Bitch, or Hoe, or anything else until I tell you to, Dealer. Now, give me all your money."

"Or what? Who are you supposed to be anyway, a terminator?"

"My name is Justice. Give me your money, now, or else."

"Or else what?" He asked as he pulled out a gun and stuck it to her head.

"Or else I'll take it off your dead body. Your call."

He pulled the trigger, but she wasn't there and the bullet went bouncing off the walls and down the street. He screamed as she broke his arm, the gun fell to the ground to be kicked aside. The other two men ran away. She slammed him face first onto the sidewalk and rifled his pockets, finding a wad of cash.

"Thanks," she said as she released him and walked away. She heard the running feet behind her and blurred out of his sight. The knife in his hand was turned against him and driven deep into his body. As he gasped in shock he was grabbed from behind and his neck snapped. Again she walked away. "Some guys just never learn," she muttered as she returned to the subway platform.

Tasha rode to a shopping area, bought some of what she needed, then returned. After the train pulled away, she hopped onto the tracks and walked back to the hidden entrance of her hideout. Stepping through the door she sensed someone was there.

Carefully lowering her treasures to the steps, she began to search the place. She found him sleeping in the old car. It was the guy who'd led her to this hideout. His name was Freddy. Tasha nudged him with her foot. "Hey Freddy."

Startled awake, he came to his feet swinging. To her surprise, he was fast and deadly. Without her superpowers she would have been killed. "Whoa, there, big fella, it's me, runaway Tasha. Cut it out." She'd blocked all his blows but hadn't retaliated.

"Huh? Shit, I'm sorry kid. Did I hurt you?"

"Nope. Scared the crap out of me, but no harm done. You hungry?"

"Yeah, I am. Got anything to drink?"

"Just water, will that do?"

"Yeah. I'm supposed to be on the wagon anyway. Cripes it's dark in here. Got any candles?"

"Just a minute, I'll light the place up then we'll share a sandwich."

He listened carefully as she walked away, retrieved some packages, and then returned. "Are you blind, girl?"

"No. Why did you ask that?"

"Because it's pitch dark in here and you walk around like you know where you're going. Only a blind person could do that."

"Yeah, well, I can see in the dark."

"Right."

"No, I really can. Hang on now, I'll switch on the lights." Suddenly a bright beam of light sprang to life. She pushed aside her packages and sat on the floor, patting the space near her. He sat. She handed him a sandwich and bottle of water. "So tell me, Freddy. Why did you bring me here in the first place?"

"You're on the run. That's easy to see." He spoke around a mouthful of sandwich. "But it was for the music."

"The music?"

"On your shoulders. You have the treble clef on one shoulder and the bass on the other. It's been a long time since I heard real music. I hoped you had some with you. You know, real music made by real people. Not that canned shit I hear on the car radios up on the street."

"Really. So you're a music lover. Do you play?"

"Long ago and far away."

"What do you play?"

Piano, guitar, some drums. You?"

"Flute. All I have with me is a tin whistle. I'll play some in a while, but first I have a few questions for you."

"You're too young to be a cop, girl. What's your gig?"

"You wouldn't believe me if I told you."

"Try me."

"Okay. I'm a priestess of Moragah, goddess of wisdom and defender of the weak. I've been granted superpowers so I can bring justice to people who have seen none of it."

"Justice? Is that what it is? I heard cops up topside asking around for anyone with your tattoos. They said you shot your parents then killed a police sergeant when you broke out of jail."

"Yeah? Did they mention how I got my hands on a police pistol to kill my parents with?"

"No, but I noticed you packing one when I brought you down here."

"Yes you did. I took it off the sergeant when I killed him. Listen, the cops broke into our house, shot Mom and Dad, and then tore the place apart looking for me. It was me they wanted. They were going to kill me in the jail and make it look like a suicide. Moragah came to me; made me a priestess and I escaped."

"That's your story?"

"It is. So what's your story?"

"I served two tours overseas then came home to find my job had been shipped out to China. To top it off they had me listed as dead and my widow had already cashed in the life insurance. I had trouble shaking the crazy, the nightmares, and voices in my head. I couldn't find work; started drinking heavy, and here I am. There was no justice for me, girl.

"So you have super powers. What can you do?"

Tasha chuckled then stood up. "You already know I can see in the dark. You know I'm fast enough to block you and not get hurt. I'm really strong too. Come on, I'll show you." She led him outside then his jaw dropped as she lifted up one end of the old subway car.

"Now, here's another one. Close your eyes, count to ten and I'll hide. Use the light, try to find me." He nodded and closed his eyes. After a thorough search of the area he gave up. "Right here, Freddy," she smiled as she stepped away from the side of the car.

"Damn, girl. That's a trick worth the learning. I could have used that overseas."

"I'll bet."

"So, what's the story on justice? You're not likely to find any of that in this country, not anymore."

"I'm not looking to find it, Freddy. I'm here to bring it. First I'm going to find out what really happened with my parents. Why they were killed, why the cops wanted me dead, and what the heck was on my cell phone that started it all."

"Okay, what happens then, girl?" he asked, sinking to the concrete floor and resting his back against the rusty wheel of the subway car.

"When I find out why, then I'll know who. And then they die."

"Sounds reasonable to me."

"It does?"

"Girl, I have seen shit, and done shit, all in the name of a system that destroyed me, lied to me, and then threw me away. They trained me to kill without conscience, but it didn't work, not completely. Look, I've drunk myself into oblivion dozens of time to quiet the voices in my head, to stop the nightmares. I've stood up on the top of the bridge deciding if I wanted to jump or not a few times too. Let me help you, girl. If I get gunned down in the process, well, it's no great loss to the world."

Tasha gazed at him for a moment then closed her eyes and called. "Moragah, did you hear?"

"I heard, my priestess," came that motherly voice as the vast presence of Moragah surrounded her, engulfed her in feelings of well being.

"Can I trust him?"

"You can. The man is intensely loyal, and he's chosen you for that. However, he believes you're just another hallucination."

"Can you help him?"

"Yes. I believe this man will make a strong ally for you. Reach out and take his hand."

"Freddy, look at me." Tasha smiled as she reached for his hands.

As they touched the presence of Moragah enfolded him like a mother's arms, sweeping aside all fears, trauma, pain, and delusions, restoring him to his prime mentally. "Holy shit," he gasped.

"Actually, my name is Moragah," came a soft chuckle in his mind. "I would make a bargain with you, Frederick Eccles. Will you bargain with me?"

"I'll do anything you want. Anything at all." He sighed as his body and mind relaxed completely for the first time since he entered military training.

"I've restored you for the moment. Assist Tasha as best you can, and I'll make this permanent. Is it a deal?"

"Deal. Oh god yes, it's a deal."

"Then so be it. Welcome to the bloodline." At that Moragah withdrew from him, leaving him bewildered, but clear and fully alert for the first time in years.

"Holy shit."

"Actually," grinned Tasha, "that's Holy Moragah. I believe she mentioned that to you."

"She did, yes. Sorry. I just... Wow, this is the best I've felt in years. What did she mean, welcome to the bloodline?"

"As I understand it, when Moragah makes a priestess, as she did with me, that girl has to find allies. Those people who are completely loyal to the priestess are called the bloodline. They don't have superpowers like the priestess, but they help her where they can. That's the deal you made."

"I'll keep my word, girl. I swear I will."

"You know that in the eyes of the law I'm planning murder."

"No, you're planning justice. I've killed people before, and it messed me up because there really was no good reason for it. This will be different."

"Leave the dirty work to me, Freddy. You've done your service."

"So, what's my job, Lady Justice?" He grinned at her and she smiled in return.

"Lady Justice. I like that. Freddy, you're my infiltrator on the street. You can fit in; learn what the street folk know."

"Not a problem, Boss. I think you're going to need another infiltrator though. One who can function topside."

"Yeah. I think I just might know who we can get. I think I know an honest cop. We'll see if we can track her down tomorrow."

Time to Start Digging

Next morning Freddy arose from the bed of cardboard and stretched. He hadn't felt that good in years. Tasha was already gone. He grinned with pleasure as he spotted the food she'd left for him. "All right, soldier, eat fast then get topside. Lady Justice needs intel and you're the guy who has to gather it." He was still savouring the chocolate bar as he sauntered into the mission.

While Freddy was hanging around the mission, listening to the street folks chat about the latest happenings on the street, Tasha was back in the area of her old home. She'd had a slight pang as she passed by the old high school. Ah well, those days were long gone, so was college now.

Taking up a post near the house, she settled down to wait. After several hours with nothing happening, she went to investigate. The place was behind police tape and locked up tight. Even her bedroom window was close and locked. Well, crap," she muttered as she dropped back to the ground. Maybe they're watching the graveyard.

She set out at a jog, but an hour later she stopped to rest. Even a super powered priestess could run out of gas. "Ah, face it, Tasha, we're out of shape." She sighed. Downing the last drop from her water bottle, she set out again. Fifteen minutes later she arrived at the graveside of her parents. There was no one near. Gazing at the cold stone, she broke down and cried.

It was hours later, and the day was wearing on when she finally rose to her feet, said good-bye, and set out again. This day's a bust," she complained to no one in particular. "Might as well go home." She headed back towards the nearest subway station.

Tired and hungry, Tasha decided to stop in at the supermarket for some food and water. As she entered the building she heard a terrified woman screaming, pleading. There was a burly policeman, trying to drag a black woman towards the doors. "Please, Sir, please. Just let me call my sister to come get my children, please." The two small children tried to pull their distraught mother out of the man's hands.

"I just want to check your ID. I need you to come outside with me. The kids can stay here for a few minutes."

"No, I won't leave my children, please let me call my sister to come get them. I can show you my ID right here."

"I need to check your ID outside by my car, now let's fucking go." He snarled as he yanked hard on her arm. "Are you resisting arrest?" His day went all to hell from there.

"Let her go," came a soft feminine voice.

The big cop took one look at Tasha and snorted in derision. "Bugger off, kid before I haul you in for interfering with a policeman."

Tasha said nothing as she pulled a stick of greasepaint out of her pocket and drew a spiral on her forehead, left cheek, and then the right. "What has this woman done? What probable cause do you have to manhandle this woman and terrorize her children? You said arrest, are you arresting her? On what charge?"

"Why you little shit, when I'm done with this one, I'm coming back for you."

"I said let her go. Let her go and walk away."

"What the fuck have you been smoking, kid?" He jerked the woman's arm again and Tasha moved. Her fist sank into his huge belly and the air whooshed from his lunges. He staggered back against the wall, trying desperately to get air back into his lungs.

"Ma'am, take you kids and go home now. This man won't bother you anymore."

"Who are you?"

"My name is Justice. You go ahead now. Take these guys home where they'll be safe."

Before the woman could move Tasha heard the policeman behind her. "You fucking little bitch, I'm taking you in for assaulting a police officer and for obstructing justice." The tazer hit her full force.

The jolt barely registered on her as she jerked the electrodes away. "I'm Justice. Now you're pissing me off. Back away and let these people leave or I'll hurt you bad."

"The hell you will." He snarled as his gun leaped to his hand. He had no target he could see. She blurred into motion, a heavy blow struck his arm causing him to drop the gun, then another blow struck his jaw and he fell, his neck broken. "You'd shoot a gun in a store full of people? You stupid ass." Tasha snarled as she reappeared, breathing deeply.

She took his gun and spare magazine then reached for his radio. "I wonder how this thing works." She pushed the button and spoke. "Hello, can anybody hear me?"

"Who is this? What are you doing with a police radio?"

"My name is Justice. I'm letting you know that a policeman attacked me, and I killed him. His body is at the market on East Seventeenth. You might want to come pick him up." With that she tossed the radio aside. "All right ma'am, take your kids and go home."

The woman was looking at her, terrified. "You killed him."

"Yes I did. Would you have preferred I just walk by and let him drag you outside for whatever he was going to do? I don't think so. He was in the wrong, I asked him to let you go, and he attacked me. I killed him in self defence. Now, take the kids home before any more cops show up here."

"Okay, yes, we're going. Come on kids, we have to hurry. You run girl, don't let them catch you." She hurried out with her children running beside her.

Tasha turned to the store to see several faces staring at her. "Did any of you folks call nine-one-one while that was going down? No? Thanks for that. Look, when the police get here tell them I was attacked first, not that it will matter to them. I'll just be on my way now." She turned and walked through the door as the sirens grew closer.

Two police cars skidded to a halt just outside the Market. With guns drawn the men raced into the building. Moments later the ambulance arrived, the body was brought out and the police began a search of the area. Two of them walked by the girl standing in the shadows at the corner of the parking lot. She nodded as she heard them talking.

"Good Jesus, this must be the same kid that killed the sergeant."

"Probably."

"How many of us do you think she'll get before we get her?"

"How the hell should I know? What's the matter, you getting nervous?"

"Maybe I am. You heard what they said in there. That kid was unarmed, and she took down Bronson. That guy was built like a tank and wearing body armor."

"Yeah, I heard them."

"This is all your goddam fault, Murdock."

"My fault?"

"You shot her parents but didn't get her. You fucked it up."

"I fucked it up? Where you there? Where you? No, you were out harassing teenage girls. Shut the hell up and keep looking."

"So, that's what you look like, Officer Murdock. Maybe I'll just go hang around the precinct until you're off duty. We need to talk." Tasha retreated deeper into the shadows.

The search turned up nothing and eventually they returned to the station house. Bill Murdock finished his shift then got in his car and drove across town to his modest house. He parked in the driveway then disappeared inside. He hadn't noticed the cab follow him home, nor did he see a shadowy figure slip out of the cab before it turned and drove away. He took a bottle of whiskey from the cupboard and poured himself a drink.

Alicia Murdock arrived home a couple of hours later to find her father sleeping on the couch, the half empty bottle beside him. With a sigh she carefully removed the bottle and reapplied the cap. She was in the business of returning the whiskey to the cupboard when he roused. "Hey, Al, bring that back here."

"Dad, you're drunk already."

"Not quite, but working on it, son. Gimme back my bottle, there's a good boy."

"Dad, please don't do this." Alicia looked crushed and he relented, albeit with little grace. "Fine, Alicia, please give back my bottle of whiskey. There's a good girl. Is that better?"

"It's a start." She sighed as she passed back the bottle and watched him pour another drink. "All right, tell me what happened?"

"That damned kid got another guy today. Christ, I saw the security tapes before they erased them."

"Who erased security tapes?"

"Hobson. It was Bronson again. He had some black woman and was trying to drag her outside away from her kids. She was hysterical. That's when the Stewart kid showed up. She told Bronson to leave off and he went after her. He had his gun out and she took him down."

"And that has you drinking because...?"

"They set me up, Al. I mean Alicia. They're all blaming me for killing that kid's parents. She'll be coming for me any day now. Don't worry; I've got lots of insurance. You'll be fine. You can sell the house and..."

"Dad, please don't talk like that."

"You have to face the reality. I don't know how she does it, but if that kid comes for me I'm a goner."

"No you're not," came a soft voice from the shadows. "At least not yet." Alicia had plastered herself against the wall and Murdock went for his gun. It wasn't where it was supposed to be; it was in Tasha's hand.

"So this is it," sighed Murdock as he relaxed back on the couch. "Go ahead, do it. Maybe it'll make you feel better."

"It won't," replied Tasha as she handed the now empty gun to Alicia. "It just makes me feel sick. "Tell me, Officer Murdock; were you even at my house that night?"

"Yeah, I was there, but I didn't shoot your parents, and I can prove it to you."

"Go ahead, I'm listening."

"I was outside keeping watch on the back of the house. I saw you stick a leg out the window then there were shots inside. Somebody yelled my name then you went out the window and climbed onto the roof. I was left there to watch the house. You didn't come down until the cars had all gone."

"Well, that settles that." Tasha sighed as she passed the bullets for the gun to Alicia. "That's what happened, and there's no way you could know where I went unless you saw me. Also, you didn't rat me out.

"I'm half starved; got anything to eat?"

"Doubt it," replied Murdock. "Want a drink?"

"Sure." Tasha grinned and winked at Alicia. "Got any bottled water?"

"I'll get you some and something to eat," said Alicia as she offered the gun back to Tasha.

"Thanks." Tasha smiled as she took the gun and passed it back to Murdock.

He just rolled his eyes and tossed it aside on the couch. "Al, make an old drunk some coffee?"

"Love to," replied the voice from the kitchen, "as soon as you remember my name."

"Oh for fuck sake. Alicia, please make your old dad some coffee."

"Working on it."

"So, I take it the gender change is new," said Tasha as she lowered herself into a chair.

"Yeah. I made him..."

"Her."

"Her, wait until university before doing the change."

"Why?"

"Why? To keep her alive, that's why. You know what this city's like. You know what the people I work with are like."

"Yeah, I know." At that point Alicia returned with sandwiches, water, and coffee for her father.

"Thanks." Tasha dove in with a will. The sandwiches didn't last long. "Oh god, that feels so much better." Tasha sighed as she finished the water. "So, you're in Uni. What's your major?"

"I'm shooting for a career as an investigative journalist. You in music?"

"That was the plan. How did you know?"

"The tats on your shoulders were a dead giveaway. So, what do the spirals stand for?"

"Long story."

"We've got time, right dad?"

"Okay, I'll talk. I was just like every other kid a week or so ago, trying to find where I fit in, and looking for a way to change the world."

"Yeah, I get that." Murdock waved a hand for her to continue.

"Anyway, the cops came busting into the house and killed my parents then tried to blame me for it. I went to a lawyer who talked me into giving myself up. Bad idea. It seems it was my cell phone they wanted.

"They let me go, followed me, and then took me back in. The officer who took me in made sure I was still alive. She wanted to stay the night, but the sergeant sent her home. Then he started talking with somebody else about how to kill me and make it look like suicide.

"That's when I remembered about Moragah, goddess of wisdom, defender of the weak. I prayed to her, and she came to me. She made me a priestess and gave me superpowers."

"Right," snorted Murdock.

"Okay, smart ass, you tell me how I do what I do then."

"I have no idea at all, girl."

"I just told you. Pay attention. So, the spiral sign is sacred to Moragah. I wear it to honor her, especially when I'm going into battle."

"Battle?"

"What else would you call it, Officer Murdock? My family has been murdered, my life ruined, and now I'm the object of a manhunt. I plan to fight back. No, it's going to be a battle. I will tell you this; I'm a priestess of Justice. I deliver justice where none will exist otherwise. That's what happened to the last guy."

"Bronson. Yeah, no doubt at all he had it coming. I don't even want to think about what he had in store for that poor woman. Okay, so let's say I swallow this story of yours, what am I supposed to do about you?"

"You've got two options here. One, try to capture me and face the results of that."

"Or?"

"Help me. Help me find justice for my family. Help me root out the power-hungry murders masquerading as police."

"They are the police, kid."

"Yeah? Whatever happened with, *to serve and protect*?"

"Long gone, kid. It's, *to uphold the law* now."

"You're kidding."

"Nope. When I first joined the force the idea was to hire peacekeepers. To serve and protect. Last few years they've been hiring enforcers, military mindset types. To uphold the law at any cost. Fuck it. I just have eighteen months more to survive then I can retire and get far away from here. Go someplace where there's nothing to do but fish."

"So, does that mean you'll help me or not?"

"Not. Kid there's nothing I can do for you that wouldn't cost me my life."

"I'll help you, if I can," Alicia said softly.

"Al, no..."

"Dad, yes. You said they tried to set you up with this in case it went sideways. Now they're trying to hang it on this girl. I'm sorry; I didn't catch your name."

"Tasha. Now they call me Lady Justice. I like it better."

"I do understand the preferring of a new name. All right, Justice, how can I help?"

"Now just hold on here," sighed Murdock. "All right, I'll do what I can; just keep Alicia out of it."

"No way, Dad, I'm in. We're both in."

"All right, I know when I'm beat, but we do this the right way."

"The hell we will," exclaimed Tasha. "No, we do this my way. I found out who ordered the death of my family. That man is dead. I need to find out who pulled the trigger then he goes down. After that I find out why. When I find who was behind it, I deliver justice. That's how it is. That's how it works. That's what I do.

"If you don't want to help me, fine. Just don't get in my way."

"Jesus, we'll all be dead in a week, kid. Ah, what the hell. I'm sick to my soul the way things are now. Seems every new guy on the force just wants to shoot something...or somebody. All right, what do you want us to do?"

"Moragah?" she called in her mind.

"I am here my priestess."

"Can I trust them?"

"You can."

"Thank you." She smiled as the vast presence pulled back to let her work. "All right, Officer. I need two things from you. First I need the name of the man who pulled the trigger on my mom and dad. Second I need the address of Officer Jessica Logan."

"Logan? What do you want with her?"

"I want to thank her for trying to keep me alive. I also want to see if I can learn anything from her. Look, don't take any chances. Don't ask questions that will alert anyone or make them wary of you. Just keep your ears open.

"Alicia, I want you to do your investigative thing. This all started when I was at that protest rally. There were lots of us there, taking selfies and other pictures. For some reason they wanted my cell phone for evidence. They were afraid I would post something damaging on the internet. I need you to find out who was at that rally with enough power to have the police go on a murder spree. Be careful; don't let anyone know what you're really doing."

"Got it. How do we contact you if we find something?"

"I'm working on that. I'll let you know when I have something set up."

Alicia nodded then her father spoke. "Okay, Lady Justice, I don't know where Logan lives, but she does a lot of volunteer work at the women's shelter on Twelfth Ave."

"Great. I'll check it out."

"I'll give you a lift."

"Alicia..."

"Dad, we have to prove our trust here. She's trusting us, now we have to return some of that."

"Just be careful, okay?"

"I will, Dad. You drink the rest of that coffee while I'm gone."

"I will, I promise." As the car pulled out of his driveway Bill Murdock poured the rest of the whiskey down the drain. He wouldn't dare have a drink now, not ever again until this was over. He needed to keep his wits about him, and he needed to keep his child alive.

"This is the place," said Alicia. She'd parked the car outside the building.

"Thanks." Tasha smiled and held out her hand. "Write your phone number on my hand. I'll contact you as soon as I get a new phone."

Alicia wrote. "Do you need any money? I have a few bucks I could..."

"No, thanks anyway, but I have a bit of money left and I can always get more."

"You can?"

"Yeah, I take it from the drug dealers, bad guys, and anybody else who gets in my face."

"Okay, good to know..."

"Hey, sorry. You have nothing to fear from me, but you know I can't get a job, bank account, or..."

"All right." Alicia nodded and smiled. "I get it. Justice, thanks."

"For what?"

"For not killing my dad for one. For not hating me on sight for another."

"Hey, I know what it's like being on the outside, not finding a place where I fit. You're all right, Sister Alicia. You're part of the bloodline now."

"The bloodline? What's that?"

"My personal friends." Tasha returned Alicia's bright smile and climbed out of the car.

New Recruit

Jessica Logan said goodnight and watched to make sure everyone was safely in their car and away before she turned to her own vehicle. Her hand barely touched the handle when a soft voice behind her spoke. "Officer Logan." She spun and lashed out. Several missed blows later she stopped and faced the grinning woman with the blue spirals on her face and forehead.

"Jesus, girl, you scared the crap out of me. Stop laughing, dammit. It's not funny."

"Sorry." Tasha was still grinning.

"No you're not," growled Jessica. She sighed and leaned back against the side of her car. "I've been expecting you to show up."

"Yeah? How come?"

"Who else could you trust? Everyone you ever knew is under surveillance. I'm about all you have left."

"You're pretty sharp, Officer Logan."

"Thanks, I do try. So, you want to tell me how you took down those two officers?"

"It's a bit of a story. You want to talk it over out here or in your car?"

"All right, in the car." She unlocked it and they climbed inside.

"Okay, go ahead, ask me," grinned Tasha as she settled into the seat of the car. A while later she finished her tale, leaving out any reference to Murdock and his daughter.

"A priestess huh."

"Don't believe me? Got a better explanation?"

43

"None at all, girl. Okay, so what's the endgame here? What are you planning to do?"

"Find the man who pulled the trigger on my family then he dies. After that, I want the man who set this all in motion. Same endgame there. Once I have justice I plan to bring justice wherever I see the need."

"So now you're a vigilante?"

"Call it what you want, but you know damn well the police in this city are corrupt. Half of them are killers, and it doesn't take much to provoke them."

"They're not all like that. Not all of them, you have to believe that."

"I do believe it. You see, I believe you're one of them, one of the good ones. That's one of the reasons I came to you. I want you to help me."

"Help you kill the people I work with? Are you crazy?"

"You'd rather help them kill innocent citizens?"

"That's not what I said, girl. Don't go putting words in my mouth."

"Look, Officer Logan..."

"Jess. My friends call me Jess."

"Thanks, Jess. Look, you were willing to risk your life, and your job, to keep me alive a few more hours. You knew what was going to happen. What was your plan?"

Jessica Logan didn't speak, she just pulled into a drive through, ordered coffee and doughnuts for two then drove to a corner of the parking lot. She took a long sip from the coffee then sighed. "When Sarge sent me home I knew you were as good as dead. I went home and called Internal Affairs."

"And?"

"I was told things were already under investigation. Just shut up and lay low until it was finished. I knew then the whole damned department is rotten to the core. Don't get me wrong, there are a lot of good cops on the force, but they're afraid to speak up. They're lying low and, I guess, so am I."

"So, help me change it. Help me clear out some of them."

"Girl, you're not Batman."

"No, he's rich, lucky bugger. And anyway, this isn't his city; it's mine. So, are you in or out?"

Again, Jessica Logan was quiet for a long moment. Finally, she nodded. "Let's just say for a moment you can do this. What then? They'll never stop hunting you."

"No, they won't, but I'll be hunting them too. As long as there's a need for justice in this city I'll be there. I know evil will never stop, but neither will I, and I'm not alone."

"You mean all those stories about Lady Blue, the goddess of the streets? Urban legends, girl, nothing more."

"Oh yeah, think so? I'll introduce you to a legend next time she's in town."

"Right. Okay, what do you want from me?"

"Don't say anything and don't ask any questions that might start people wondering. Just listen, let me know if you hear of something I should know."

Tasha was surprised at what Jessica said next. "I want something from you too, Lady Justice."

"Oh?"

"Yeah, if I get anything you should look into I need to know you won't let it pass."

"All right," Tasha replied, slowly nodding her head. "If you try to set me up I'll know, and there'll be hell to pay."

"I won't, girl. I won't. Look, I joined the force to help people, but that's not easy to do these days. Internal Affairs doesn't want anything to do with it, so that leaves you. To tell you the truth, I won't be sorry to see a bit of justice delivered in this town."

"Deal, Jess. I mean that."

"So, how do I contact you?"

"I'll let you know as soon as I get something set up."

"Just no sky beacon with a J on it or anything."

That brought a smile to Tasha's face. "Actually, I was thinking more about a cell phone. Your partner shot my last one."

"Yeah. He's such a pain in the ass. Shoots every dog he sees because a poodle bit him when he was a kid. Dipshit. So, you got a place to stay?"

"Just drop me at the subway station."

"Subway station coming up." Jessica pulled the car into gear and drove away.

Lay of the Land

F reddy woke to see her sleeping on the bed of cardboard he'd made for her. He grinned and slipped away, going topside to the mission for a meal and a chance for a shower and change of clothes. With his mind completely clear, he noticed things. One thing was that the street folks noticed the difference. He realized he'd have to work on appearing burnt out. Okay, he'd always enjoyed little theater; time to put that hobby to use.

He spent the rest of his morning wandering around, listening to people talk, chatting with a few, especially the veterans who ended up on the streets like he had. He also scouted out a few more things. Things he thought might be useful to Lady J.

When he returned to the hideout she was gone again. Or was she? "Lady J, you here? I'm alone and wasn't followed."

"I know."

The voice came from behind him. Every nerve in his body screamed at him to react, but he fought the urge and turned to face her slowly. "Dammit, girl. You have got to stop scaring the crap out of me. I'm no good to you if I drop dead from fright."

"Sorry. Got anything to eat?"

"Nope, sorry. You can get a meal at the mission soup kitchen. It's only a couple of blocks away. You can get a shower there too if you're willing to take your chances."

"Take my chances?"

"Your tats, girl. The cops have every snitch on the street looking for a girl with those tattoos."

Tasha sighed and sank to a cross legged position on the floor. "That sucks."

"It truly does." Freddy sank to the floor near her. "I've got some more intel. It's not golden, but it's useful."

"I'm listening."

"Okay, they're looking for you everywhere, but they're keeping somewhat quiet About it. Nobody knows why.

"On a different note. Useful intel: The mission is a couple of blocks away. They'll make you pray to Jesus before they feed you, but it's food and will keep you alive. You can get a shower there and clean your clothes but keep a close watch or everything will get stolen.

"There's a thrift store run by the mission folks another block further on. You can get fresh clothes there for a few bucks. Sometimes people from uptown go there to shop for vintage stuff or to make donations. Sit outside and play your tin whistle. You'll make enough to buy an outfit or two.

"Now for the sewers. The system is old, really old, in this part of town. Parts of it have been changed, parts closed off but not filled in, lots of different access points..."

"You think this would be a good way to get around the city, like the Ninja Turtles."

That made him laugh; something else he hadn't done in a long time. "That's it exactly, but I was thinking more like the Punisher or Spiderman..."

"I get it. So, you know your way around down here?"

He nodded then spoke softly, not making eye contact. "I do, Lady J. I spent a lot of time down here, scouting out the tunnels. You see, I wasn't always sure where I was, in America, or overseas. I'd hear voices from topside filtering down but was afraid to listen to them. I hid out, a lot, thinking I was in enemy territory."

"You were, Freddy. We both are." He'd suddenly sunk into a depression. He'd helped her when her life had gone all to hell because he'd seen and done worse. He wasn't just someone she could use; he was a friend. She wanted to cheer him up. "Hey, we need a new name for you, a code name."

He shook his head slowly then raised it to give her a sloppy grin. "A code name? Like Robin?"

"I don't know, but something. You know your way around, Mapster maybe? No, you know stuff too, how about Intel?"

"Intel," he chuckled. "Yeah, I like it. So, you're Lady Justice and I'm Intel. It's not such a bad name for an IT guy."

"IT guy?"

"Yeah, I was an IT guy for a small company before I got stupid and joined the military to fight for freedom. What a pile of bullshit. We were fighting for oil, nothing more. Anyway, when I got back the company had been swallowed up and the job shipped out to China."

"So, you're good with electronics. Good to know. Okay, Intel, I'll go see what I can scrounge for a meal then you can start teaching me the routes through the sewers."

They explored for days until he felt she could find her way around. Now it was time to get back on the trail of a killer.

Jessica Logan stopped just inside the door of her second story apartment. She could hear the water running in the shower and a sweet feminine voice singing. Gun in hand she made her way cautiously to the bathroom. As she silently slipped into the steamy room the singing stopped. "Hi Jess, welcome home." The water stopped and the door slid open. "Pass me a towel?"

"Why don't I just shoot you?"

"Because you don't want to explain to your fellow police officers why I was in your house naked. Pass me a towel?"

"Good point," groused Jessica as she put away her gun and passed the towel. "Did you raid the fridge yet?"

"Not yet, but it was on the list." Tasha grinned as she swept back her wet hair and wrapped herself in the towel. "Dear god, that hot water felt good."

"Those clothes of yours could use some too. The machine is right beside you. Use it."

"Yes, Ma'am." Tasha tossed her clothes into the machine, turned it on then followed Jessica out to the kitchen. "I got in through the open window in your bedroom. You might want to brace that, the lock's broken."

"It wasn't this morning."

"Yeah, well, about that... Say, have you eaten yet?"

"Nice change of subject, Slick." Jessica chuckled. "Go dry your hair and I'll get out of this uniform and cook something."

Tasha finished blow drying her hair, preened in the mirror for a moment, remembering how her life used to be, then returned to the kitchen, still wrapped in the towel. Jessica was busy at the stove, humming softly.

Tasha began to sing the harmony. When Jess turned and smiled, they each realized how young the other was. Tasha was just out of her teens and Jessica hadn't reached thirty yet. Somehow it seemed to bring them closer.

"You can crash on the couch for the night if you want."

"Thanks, but I have to get going. I owe you big time for the shower and the food. My clothes are dry now so I should go."

"Use the door this time."

"Yes, Ma'am. Jess..."

"Okay, I do have something for you. The guy you killed at the market? He was the trigger man. Bronson killed you parents. He and the sergeant were buddies. I don't know why they were killed yet. I do know you weren't the first, I mean, your house wasn't the only one they hit looking for cell phones. Fortunately, nobody else was hurt."

"So I got justice for mom and dad after all. Thanks for that, Jess. I'll be in touch."

"Hey, Lady J, how am I supposed to contact you if I need you? Have you set anything up yet?"

"Just put the word out on the street that Lady J needs to do the laundry. It'll get to me." With that she slipped out the door.

From the window Jessica watched her walk out onto the sidewalk and hail a cab. "She's getting money from somewhere," she mused. "I don't even want to know where. Be careful, Lady Justice."

Tasha arrived back at the hideout to find a man in a ragged military uniform guarding the passageway. "Damn," she thought. "I knew I should have used the subway tracks."

"You can't go that way, kid. There's nothing down there but rubble."

"It's a place to spend the night out of the rain. Let me by."

"No can do, kid. Go away, find another spot."

She sighed and let her shoulders sag. "Move aside or I'll move you."

His laughter was deep and rich; it brought a smile to her face. "Little girl, how do you plan to move me? I outweigh you by a buck or more."

"I have my ways."

"Oh yeah? Show me your shoulders."

"What? My shoulders? Shit, you're one of Intel's guys, right?" She unzipped her hoodie and showed him the tattoo on her shoulder.

"Intel?"

"Freddy. You a friend of his?"

"Yeah. He saved my ass a time or two. You'd be Lady Justice, the one who took down that cop who was abusing the woman and her kids. Welcome back to headquarters, Lady Justice. Hey, if Freddy can get a code name I want one too."

"That's an easy one. You're Blockade."

He was still chuckling with delight as she slipped through the opening and down to the hideout. Intel was there with two more men.

Both men looked like they had seen better days. "Care to explain what's going on?"

"Lady J, you, we, need these guys. I know them and I trust them. If we're going to do what you want to do, we need them. Please tell me you didn't hurt Joe..."

"You mean, Blockade? He let me in when I showed him my tattoos. So, who are you?"

"Name's Samuel Momosa, Ma'am."

"What is it you do that I need?"

"I hear things, lots of things, and I'm a sleight of hand artist."

"Sleight of hand artist? You mean a con man."

"I grew up in a carnival group. I distract people and I learn stuff. I hear you're wanted for multiple murders, but I know you didn't shoot your parents. A cop named Bronson did that. Him you already killed. I know you've got a contact in the police force, but nobody knows who. And they do want to know who. I hear that you were at a certain protest rally. You and several others were taking pictures where you shouldn't have."

"So you're a carnie?"

"I was once, but the war ruined that. My hands aren't steady enough anymore."

"Sam is still the master of distraction techniques, Lady J," said Intel. "We can use that."

Tasha was silent for a moment, and then called in her mind. "Lady Moragah?"

"*I am here, my priestess.*"

"Can I trust these guys? This is all getting away from me and I'm scared."

"*Be at peace, my child. These men are here to help. You can trust them.*"

"Thank you Lady Moragah. Can we talk later?"

"*Of course. You need only call.*" The presence pulled back from her.

"All right, Samuel, your new name is Decoy." He grinned with delight as she then turned to the other man.

"I'm Jake, Jake Freeman. I'm a scrounge, Lady Justice. That was my job in the military too. I find stuff, anything you need, I can find it, or make it."

"Or steal it?"

"That too as required." He matched her grin.

"Okay, so you're Finder. You can start by finding me a cell phone that can't be traced."

He pulled one out of his pocket and tossed it to her. "I thought you might want one of these. It's a prepaid. When it runs out I'll get you another."

"Okay, so you're Finder. Now, Intel. Care to enlighten me as to what the heck is going on? Why are you having a party in my private railway car?"

"Sorry if I've overstepped my bounds here, Boss, but I have my reasons."

"Care to share?"

"You may have led a somewhat normal life up to this point, but I haven't. I know what's coming for you."

"And what's that?"

"They're hunting you right now. Your picture is on the ten most wanted list, every snitch in the city is looking for you. They will use technology, dogs, informants, and whatever else they can get their hands on. You will be hunted. You will be found, and they will rain hellfire down on your head until they're sure you're dead.

"While they hunt you they will do all in their power to turn the people against you. They'll lie; bribe the media to lie, and anything else they can do to poison your existence. You'll never dare to use a bank..."

"Okay, I get it. It might surprise you to know I knew this going in. Moragah gave me a chance at life. I don't expect it to be a long one. I just want some justice for my family and for everyone else while I'm alive, and I plan to get it. So what does all this have to do with you recruiting these men?"

At this point Decoy stepped up. "Ma'am, if I may. Intel explained about your mission. What you don't know is what they did to us during training and later in the field of action. We were trained to fight, to kill, and more. We all have developed skills that we dare not use now that we're home. We're haunted by what we've done, by what we've become, how we've been treated since we came back, and what we're truly capable of when pushed too hard.

"We, and a lot of others, are condemned to lead a tortured life of bare survival on the streets. We're lost, we have no direction to follow, we have no purpose for being here anymore, and our country would rather see us disappear so they don't have to deal with the problem. Most of our families have given up on us as well.

"The point is, working for you gives us purpose again. It gives us a chance to do what we wanted to do back when we first volunteered for service; serve the people of this country, protect the freedom of the people. Like you said, we probably won't live long at this, but we can at least go out with our heads held high, knowing we fought for the greater good."

"Besides, it beats drinking myself to death or starving," grinned Finder.

Tasha gazed into the eyes of each man in turn. They were all sincere. "Wow, guys, I really didn't know... Look, I have no idea how to do any of this. Until two weeks ago I was just a kid in school looking for a career in music and attending protest marches. That's how I thought we could change the world. I guess I was pretty naïve.

"Okay, I've been completely focused on finding my family's killers that I haven't given a thought to any of this. Help me out here, what's the plan?" She sank gracefully to the floor and braced her back against the wall.

The men all sat as well. "What we hope to do," said Intel, "is give you a safe place to hide out. That's job one. This place is good. We add a watchman at the street side entrance and brace the backdoor. Should be good. We put the word out that these few blocks are off limits to street shenanigans. That means no robberies, no gangs, no snitches hanging around. We recruit a few more vets who are on the streets and lost, to help out.

"They don't have to know what the big picture is, just that this area is going to be a safe place for vets who have no other place to go. Even without your mission in life, this would be a good idea for the guys.

"The next part of the plan is for us to start scoping out the areas beyond this, seeing what we can learn, what we can do to help you. Just tell us what you need."

"Guys, I don't know what to say here. I'm grateful, I truly am, but I don't want you guys taking any chances..."

"Girl, taking chances with our lives is all we know how to do," said Finder. "I can't hold a job because of the drinking; no one would hire me anyway."

"Why not?"

"A black man with mental issues, an alcohol problem, and no fixed address? Seriously? This will give me a reason to sober up. I promise I'll sleep someplace else so the nightmares won't give us away or get anybody hurt trying to wake me up."

Tasha gazed at him for a moment then closed her eyes. "Lady Moragah?"

"*Yes, my priestess?*"

"Did you hear?"

"*I did. These men are all deeply troubled. They are sincere and extremely loyal, but they are deeply wounded on many levels. Do you want to help them as we did Intel?*"

"I do, yes. Can we?"

"We can and we shall. Bring them close and join hands with them. I will heal their bodies and minds."

Tasha opened her eyes and sighed. "All right guys, first things first. Call Blockade down here."

Grinning, Intel went to fetch the big man. He had an idea what was coming. They returned and sat next to her. "Come closer, guys, join hands."

Puzzled and a bit shy, they complied. As soon as Tasha completed the circle the vast presence of Moragah enfolded them like the arms of a loving mother. All the pain, trauma, guilt, and sorrow were swept away as was the physical pain and addictions.

"Welcome, friends of Lady Justice. I am Moragah, goddess of wisdom and defender of the weak. Tasha is my priestess of justice. I know you are aware of what you face, but I would not have you face it wounded. Swear your loyalty to Lady Justice and these healings I have performed for you will become permanent. What say you? Will you be my soldier of justice?"

Dumbfounded, they just sat, basking in the loving feelings and soaking up the joy in her presence. Finally Blockade spoke softly. "I'm in. If I take a bullet tomorrow it'll have been worth it for this. Whatever you want, need, I'm in."

"Oh yeah, me too," agreed Finder, a smile on his face.

"And me too," said Decoy. "I swear my oath and life to you, Lady Goddess, and to your priestess. My life is yours."

"Then the bargain is sealed." With a final wave of loving energy she withdrew.

"Not the bloodline, but the Soldiers of Justice," mused Tasha. "I like it. Okay guys, I'm dead beat and need to sleep. I'll just curl up in the corner over there while you guys plot and plan."

Getting Organized

Whenever she awoke all was in darkness. As soon as she lifted her head, Finder spoke. "Hey there, Lady J. I see you're awake, hungry?"

"I am, but first I need to make a run down to the washrooms at the subway platform."

"Gotcha."

"Finder, I can see in the dark, but how did..."

"Night vision goggles. I've been shopping."

"I can't wait to see all the treasure," she said, smiling, "but first, nature calls."

She trotted off, easily sidestepping the other sleeping men. She let herself out through the back door. When she returned Blockade opened it for her. The men were all awake now. "Might as well turn on the lights if everybody's up."

"Eyes!" The bright flashlights leaped to life filling the old car with light.

"Okay, everyone gets a potty break while I eat breakfast." She smiled as he held up the ration bar Finder passed to her. "After that I want to see what you guys have been up to."

There were lots of chuckles and good natured banter as they got themselves organized for the day. As soon as they were ready Finder displayed what he'd found. Two pairs of night goggles, three side arms and two automatics as well as one assault rifle. There was also ammunition and a pile of cash.

"Where did you get all this?"

"Ma'am," replied Intel, "we took it from those who shouldn't have it anyway. There were a few gangers, a wanna-be robber, a drunken wife beater, and some other miscreants. We did this to show we mean business. We explained to them all this area is a safe zone for veterans and we mean to enforce it. They were all more than willing to donate to the cause."

"I'm sure they were. Okay, guys, well done."

"All right, we're as ready as we can be," declared Intel. "Orders, Ma'am?"

Taken aback for a moment, Tasha just stared at him then caught herself. Yes, she was supposed to be in charge. She had to direct this group of men and keep them alive as long as possible while taking full advantage of their skills to help her.

"Okay, the job is still the same. I want the people who caused my family to get killed, however, I have other folks topside working on that. What I need here is a better set-up, word from the street of anything, you guys can work on your safety zone, but first I need something from you tech savvy types."

Intel chuckled at that. "What do you need?"

"I need some way to contact my people topside and for them to contact me without getting them or me busted. Can it be done?"

"It can. Finder, I'll need some stuff."

"It'll cost, or I can steal it."

"Can't you use some of that money?" asked Tasha.

"That's up to you, Ma'am. This is team money. You're team leader."

She looked at the pile of money again. There had to be thousands of dollars there. "Wow. Okay. Look, I do need a few bucks for food and cab fares. Give me fifty and do whatever you want with the rest."

Intel picked up the piles of money and passed her two hundred dollars. "I'll be the company purser, Ma'am, if that's all right with you." She nodded. "Finder, take the rest and get what you need."

"On it, Sarge." He rose easily, took the money, and then headed up the passageway to the street.

"All right, men," Intel went on. "We continue to spread the word today, forage what we can, and remember, keep this on the QT. We don't want to start some media circus or bring a lot of police attention down on us. This is full on black ops, people. Understood?"

"Understood."

They rose easily to their feet and left. Alone with her thoughts, Tasha called for Moragah.

"*I am here, my priestess. You are troubled. Why?*"

"Lady Moragah, I'm supposed to greet you at moonrise, but I'm underground most of the time after dark. How..."

"*It doesn't matter, my child. I feel your love and respect in your heart. For now that is more than enough.*"

"Would it be all right if I made a way for me and the guys to honor you?"

"*Of course. Remember your men are soldiers. Perhaps something with a military bent might be easier for them.*"

Tasha smiled with delight as she felt Moragah's pleasure and laughter. "I'll see what I can come up with."

The day was well on and darkness falling by the time the men returned to the hideout. There, just outside the door to the old subway car stood a table draped with blue cloth. There were white candles flanking a small balance scale and backed by a large piece of white pasteboard with a blue spiral on it. "So, what's this about?" asked Intel.

Tasha smiled and waved a hand at her creation. "Guys, you've all felt the presence of Moragah. You know She's real. She has healed you all and you've bargained with her. Moragah is real. This is how we'll honor her." She stood in front of the altar and made the sign of the spiral in the air. "For Moragah, for Justice. Say it with me now."

"For Moragah, for Justice!" They all stood to attention and saluted.

"Yes, my soldiers of Justice. This altar is here to remind us all of why we do what we do. For Moragah, for Justice."

"For Moragah, for Justice!"

Suddenly the presence of Moragah engulfed them, filling them with feelings of happiness and wellbeing. *"My priestess, my soldiers. This pleases me greatly. Thank you. I will grant you peaceful sleep tonight, no need to post a guard."* With that she withdrew.

"Come in guys; show me what you've got."

There were more weapons and ammunition, bags of food rations, bits and pieces of electrical equipment and three cell phones. There was more money as well. "More cash?"

"Some of the gangers came back with friends. They donated more money and weapons," replied Intel. "The word is out now, and a few vets have drifted into the area. They believe we're up to something and want to help. I'll let Finder explain the rest."

"Ma'am, these are prepaid phones The numbers are on the sides. Just tell us who gets them and if you need more."

"Actually these three will do fine. I'll distribute them."

"Need to know. Yes ma'am. Understood. Now this..."

"No, wait, you guys should know this, just in case. One of these goes to police officer Jessica Logan. One is for me, and the last is for Officer Murdock's daughter, Alicia. Murdock can contact me through Alicia as he's being watched carefully."

"Lady J, we didn't need to know that."

"Yes you did, Finder. You guys are the inner circle; you need to be kept in the loop at all times. If something goes crazy and one of those people came looking for me, you need to know they can be trusted."

"Yes, Ma'am. Thank you for that. Okay, now, this pile of magic will become electric lights in here as well as surveillance cameras on all approaches to headquarters."

"Sweet. Did you notice that there is no electricity down here?"

"Not a problem," grinned Intel. "The subway runs on electricity. We'll just borrow some; they'll never even notice it's gone."

"You guys are amazing, you know that? Okay, I'll leave you to it while I do phone delivery. Have fun guys."

Building the Net

Tasha tried to find Alicia, but eventually had to give up. Several people had begun to give her strange looks. Damn. Okay, back to headquarters for some help. Next day she went out again.

Alicia Murdock was trying, and failing, to act normal as she hurried out of city hall and walked back to her car. She was almost to her car when she felt a bump that knocked her against the side of a van.

"Sorry, Miss." The man in the ragged military jacket mumbled an apology as he took her arm to steady her. He released her without making eye contact and shuffled down the street. Raising a cell phone close to his lips he spoke softly. "Package delivered." He then switched it off.

Half frightened, Alicia got in her car and drove home. Something about that encounter with the street person was bothering her. As she pulled in the driveway it hit her. He'd been using a cell phone. "Oh my god, my phone!"

She parked the car and grabbed her purse. A frantic search showed her phone to be right where it was supposed to be. She sighed in relief then got out, locked up, and let herself into the house. As she hung up her coat she felt a soft bump. She was reaching for the pocket when it suddenly buzzed.

Startled, Alicia jerked her hand away, then, tentatively looked inside. There was another cell phone in that pocket. Hesitantly, she answered it. "Hello?"

"Hi Alicia, it's Justice. Got your new phone I see."

Alicia laughed. "Yeah. The street guy, he didn't steal anything, he gave me a present."

"Yep, that was Decoy. He's a friend. My number is on the side of the phone. Keep it secret, but you can use it to contact me if you need to."

"What if I just want to?"

Tasha laughed with delight. "Hey, that would be okay too. So, you got time for a coffee with a buddy?"

"Sure. Where and when?"

"Your place, right now. Just open up and let me in." The phone went dead and a soft knock came on the door.

Alicia smiled as she opened the door and ushered Lady Justice in. She seated her guest then set about making coffee. "So, Lady J, what's the deal with the phones?"

"I'm the fox and the hounds are everywhere, watching, listening. I thought it best to keep our connection secret. I don't want to put you or your dad in any danger."

"Danger? You're the one in danger. Girl, they're looking everywhere for you. Dad says there are some very nervous people on the force right now."

"Really? Well, that is good to know. It means I'm doing my job. Thanks." She accepted the steaming mug from Alicia's hand and took a sip. "Did you find out anything about that protest rally?"

"It's really kind of weird. That was a potentially volatile situation, but the Police commissioner's wife was there with him. There was another young woman there too. I don't know what she was about, but she sure caused a fuss with the commissioner's security. She may be the key to this whole thing. I'll keep digging."

"Okay but be careful; I don't want anything to happen to you."

Alicia smiled with delight as she raised her cup to her lips, took a sip, then returned it to the coffee table. "I'll be careful; I promise. However, I do have to confess, I'm enjoying this. I know this is what I want to do with my life."

"It can't be an easy way to make a living. Dangerous too at time, I'll bet."

"Yeah, I know it will be...is. That's another reason Dad had a fit when I came out as trans."

"Oh?"

"He says it's a dangerous enough for a man, far worse for a woman, and a death sentence for a trans woman."

"He's concerned for you. I get that. So why is it more dangerous for a trans woman?"

"Dad says there's a guy on the force who has killed three trans women in the past two years. One was shot and the other two were beaten to death while the man's partner just looked away."

"Oh man, that sucks. I want that man's name." Tasha set down her mug and rose to go. "Alicia, you be extra careful and keep that cell phone close. Don't hesitate to call if you need me, okay?"

Alicia rose and followed Tasha to the door. "I will, I promise. You be careful too, Lady J."

"Always." Tasha smiled and gave Alicia's arm a gentle squeeze then sauntered away looking like every other person her age, walking along staring at her phone. Except she wasn't. The phone was turned off.

It was late when Jessica Logan got home from an overtime shift. She entered her apartment and noticed a new cell phone on her kitchen table. She picked it up, glanced at the number taped to the side then dropped it into her pocket. She kicked off her shoes and drew her gun.

Carefully, she slipped through the apartment. She found Tasha asleep on her bed. With a grin of pure mischief she put away the gun and took out the new cell phone. She thumbed it on and punched in the number taped to the side. The phone in Tasha's pocket vibrated; Tasha exploded from the bed landing in a defensive stance, her eyes searching everywhere.

Jessica howled with laughter, causing Tasha to blush deeply. Tasha shook a threatening finger at her. "Think that's funny, do you?"

"Oh god, yes I do."

"I'll get you back for that, mark my words." Jessica just grinned at her. "Fine. Just for that you have to feed me."

"Okay, I guess that's fair. Come on out to the kitchen. We can talk while I cook." She led the way back to the kitchen and began to fuss about, building a meal for them. "The phone is for us to stay in touch, right?"

"Right. I really wanted that big scales of justice in the sky thing, but you wanted something more subtle. Hence the phones."

"I'm not in possession of stolen goods, am I?"

"Nope. These are legal, bought and paid for."

"Where'd you get the money?"

"I'm not telling you that. You're a policewoman for god's sake."

Jessica smiled at that then set a plate of stir fry before Tasha. "So, you've dealt with the trigger man and the guy who ordered the killings. What now?"

"Now I keep digging. There's more to this than we know right now."

"There always is." Jessica lowered herself to the chair facing Tasha. She played with her food for a minute then sighed.

Tasha finished her meal then set the fork aside. "What's on your mind, Jess?"

"I hesitate to ask, Tasha, but..."

"Hey there, buddy of mine, that's part of our deal. Ask away. Tell me what's up."

"Thing is, I'm not sure you can do anything about this. I know I can't."

"Talk already. Don't make me beat up the cook."

Jessica smiled then went on. "Okay. It's my partner being an asshole again. There is a woman who put in a call for police assistance. It was the third time in two weeks. Domestic violence call. She's got a restraining order, but..."

"It doesn't restrain the guy?"

"No indeed. We showed up today and ran the guy off, again..."

"But?"

"Here's the asshole part, Tash. This city has an ordinance saying a person can be evicted from their home for making nuisance calls to emergency services. You know, fire hall, hospital, police, etc. Anyway, this woman's three calls put her in that category. Martin went to her landlord and bullied him into evicting the woman. Noon tomorrow."

"That's the reason for her eviction? She wants protection from a violent man?"

"Yeah. She's lived there for ten years, never even been late with the rent."

"So that partner of yours; what crawled up his ass and died?" Tasha was outraged now and letting it show. Jessica didn't respond, she just looked away. "Right, let me guess. The woman is just a useless nigger bitch and a nuisance. Her man was just putting her in her place. Am I right?"

Jessica sighed again. "Yeah, that's pretty much it."

"That dirty rotten son of a bitch. God! I am so going to burn his ass. Have you got an address?" Jessica retrieved a writing pad from the end of the table and wrote out the address. Tasha stared at it for a moment then sighed. "This better not be a set up..."

Jessica's eyes went hard and her back straightened. "If you ever want a bed and a meal again that will be the last time you say anything like that to me."

Tasha met her eyes for a long moment then she relaxed back into her chair. "Apologies, Jess. My bad. Never again, I promise. I should know better than to insult the cook."

Jessica's eyes opened wide and her mouth formed a perfect O. "That's it for you, Miss Freeloader. You get out of here right now." With a laugh of delight Tasha danced towards the door. Jessica followed. "Tasha, you be careful girl. That man's trigger happy."

"I will, Jess, I promise. You phone in sick tomorrow. I don't want you getting caught in the middle of this." With that she was gone.

Jessica went to the window and watched until Tasha disappeared into a cab. "I sure hope she's getting all that money from the bad guys." She went to the bedroom to change, and the new cell phone began to buzz. She grinned as she read the text. "Ty 4 the meal. U r a great cook."

Side Job

Tasha arrived back at the hideout to find herself not in a street girl's hideout, but in a military camp on full alert. A man she didn't know stepped into her path as she headed for the ally entrance. "sorry, Kid, you can't.."

"Stand down, soldier. This woman is Lady Justice. She's a VIP guest here anytime she decided to come by for a visit." Blockade grinned as he winked at her. "Right this way, Lady J. I'll show you the way in."

Once they were inside she gripped his huge arm lightly. "Blockade, what's going on? Who was that guy?"

"One of many, Ma'am. The word is out on the streets now. This area is a safe haven for veterans and the vets keep it that way. Sadly, one of the gangs took offense to our carving out a piece of their territory. They came to do a drive by shooting to teach us a lesson. They had no real idea what they were dealing with."

"What happened?"

"We expected something like this, so we were prepared. Finder scrounged some stuff. We made a few bombs and grenades. When they started shooting we went on the offensive. The burned out cars are just down the street. The bodies have been removed to the sewers. By morning the cars will be gone too.

"Ma'am, I know you don't like this, but the message has to be clear. This is veterans territory now. You bring harm here; you don't go back. I know you probably don't..."

"No, no. It's a good policy, clean, simple, and just. Thanks for covering for me up there."

The big man chuckled at that. "No problem. I figured you don't want it known you're a permanent resident here."

At that point they arrived at the train car. The place was empty. They greeted Moragah then went inside. Blockade settled down with his hat over his eyes. Tasha pulled out her tin whistle and began to play a haunting melody. He pushed up his hat, smiled broadly, and then began to beat out the time on the side of his leg. Soon his deep voice began to pop out sounds like a bass guitar. She grinned and switched to a more lively tune. All too soon they were interrupted by the voices outside. "For Moragah; for Justice!"

Tasha stopped playing as they entered. "Hey Intel. Looks like you had some excitement."

"We did, Ma'am, but we were ready for them. Did Blocakade give you a report?"

"He did. You?"

"Then you have the bones of it. We were attacked. The insurgents were repelled, and the field of operations has been policed. The remains are well away in the main storm sewer. The rats will clean any bones that don't get washed out to sea."

"Then we're clear to go?"

"We are, Ma'am. Do you have a mission in mind?"

"I do. Listen to this..." Tasha told them about the woman being stalked and harassed by her ex. She told them about how and why the woman was being evicted.

Intel just shook his head. "This is just wrong on so many levels. What's the mission?"

Tasha sighed and leaned back against the wall. "I show up and make it stop, somehow."

"Want back-up?"

"I want you guys to stay safe."

That made them laugh. "Trust us. We're professionals," said Decoy, a broad grin on his face.

"You're all nuts. Look guys, just make it look like you're not with me, okay?"

"Now why would we do that?" asked Blockade.

"Come on, guys, you know why. You've staked out a territory here. The cops will pretty much ignore you same as they do with all the other gangs. If they get the idea you're hiding me they'll blast their way in here. People will get hurt, innocent people. I don't want that."

Intel just grinned. "No indeed, Ma'am. That would be bad. What do you think, guys? We set up an ambush?" The others nodded their agreement. "Ambush."

"All right, got an address for us?" Tasha passed it to him. Intel memorized it then passed it back. "That's at the edge of our territory anyway. All right men, let's go get set up. Dawn's coming. Ma'am, we'll be there, but we'll stay back unless needed."

They were at the door when she stopped them. "Guys, if there's a policewoman with him, don't hurt her. She's a friend. She's one of us."

"Good to know. We'll be there." With that they were gone, leaving her to get a few hours sleep. Tasha didn't need an alarm anymore. She just automatically awoke at the right time. Another superpower she enjoyed. She closed her eyes and instantly drifted away.

The tall woman stepped out of her house, glanced around nervously, and locked her door. "The place is locked," she said loudly. "There's nothing of any real value inside. I've set the alarms."

The street girl who'd been hanging around all morning looked at her and smiled. "I'm not going to break into your house. I'm here to protect you."

"Protect me? From who?"

"The police."

"The police? Why...?"

"Here they come. Stay calm. I'll take care of this." She slouched over and stuck her hands in her pockets as she pretended to shuffle away. The police cruiser lurched to a halt followed closely by another car. The woman's landlord got out of his car and a big policeman climbed out of the cruiser.

"Mr. Singh, what's going on?"

"Just shut your mouth; we'll do the talking." The big cop swaggered right up to her, getting into her personal space, and leaning forward aggressively. "You're being evicted. You've got ten minutes; go pack your shit and get out."

Frightened, the woman backed away from him. "Evicted? Why? I paid my rent. Mr. Singh?"

"I said shut up, bitch. You're being evicted for making nuisance calls to the police."

"What??? I called for help. I..."

"Okay, that's enough," came a soft female voice. Tasha had been standing right there but had gone completely unnoticed. "Back off."

Startled, the big cop spun around and went for his gun, but his hand froze above it. "Sweet Jesus, it's you."

"Yeah, it's me, but my name's Justice, not Jesus. Now back off or pay the price." He swallowed hard, but backed away, his hand moving away from the gun. "Good boy. Now, you know what I'm capable of, so just stand there and be quiet while I sort this out. Got it?" He swallowed again and, not trusting his voice, nodded that he understood.

Tasha turned to the other man. "Mr. Singh is it?"

"Yes, that is my name."

"Tell me, why would you evict a good paying tenant who has been with you for a long time?"

"That policeman told me I had to because she is causing a nuisance. I don't want to evict her."

"The police lied to you, Sir. You're under no obligation to evict this woman if you don't want to. I suggest you tear up that eviction notice right now." He didn't move, but his gaze went to the policeman for direction. The cop wouldn't meet his eyes.

"As you can see, Mr. Singh, this man is afraid of me. He has good reason. I put this to you for the last time. Tear up that eviction notice and drive away; forget any of this ever happened." He looked to the policeman again then tore up the notice and got back in his car. Tasha waited until he was gone before she spoke again.

"Now then, Officer Martin Johnson, you're a puzzle to me. You're a trigger-happy piece of work and a natural bully. You enjoy throwing your weight around to show how tough you are, but you're hiding behind that uniform. You're not as tough as you want people to believe.

"So here's the deal. You drive away and write this up as the landlord changed his mind. I promise this woman will stop calling the police. I will personally have a chat with the man harassing her. The whole thing ends here. Is it a deal?"

"What are you going to do to him?"

"I can't tell you that; you're a cop. Jeez." In spite of himself a smile touched his lips. "So, is it a deal?"

"Deal, and I never saw you. You were never here."

"Deal. Martin, I hear of you shooting dogs again I'll be pissed."

"Kid, who or what are you anyway? I mean..."

"I'm a priestess of Moragah, goddess of wisdom and protector of the weak. I work through her, that's how I can do what I do. This is my city now. I'll always be here; I'll always be watching. My name is Justice."

Martin Johnson swallowed hard again then turned away and got into his car. The sooner he got away from her the better. She was different now; not the terrified kid he'd helped haul off to jail. Now she was a super powered killer. He'd seen the video of her taking down the sergeant.

As the police car sped away the woman's voice sounded behind her. "Who are you?"

"I just explained that," replied Tasha, her eyes following the police car until it was out of sight. She turned to face the woman. "My name is Justice. You're safe now. Your home is safe. Tell me about the man abusing you?"

"Wait, what...?" Her arms fell limply to her sides, and she began to weep. "They were going to throw me out onto the street? I..."

Tasha's arms were instantly around her. As she held the weeping woman she was startled to see three heavily armed soldiers step out of hiding, salute her, then walk away.

The woman gave Tasha a gentle squeeze then stepped back, wiping at her tears. "I'm sorry, so sorry. Thank you. You've saved my home. My name is Amelda Bradley. What can I do for you? Are you hungry? Can I get you something to eat?"

"Oh gods, yes," Tasha replied, a bright smile on her face.

The smile dispelled the aura of danger that surrounded her and the woman relaxed. She took Tasha by the hand and practically dragged her into the house. "Come in so I can feed you, girl. You look half starved." She took Tasha to the kitchen and pointed her to the table. "You sit right there while I fix us something to eat."

"Tell me about the guy abusing you."

"It didn't actually get to the point of violence. I was married to a sweetheart of a man, but he was killed in Iraq. That was a few years ago. I got lonely for adult company and...oh, I'm sorry I..."

"Hey, I'm not that young. Jeez, I know about sex and all kinds of fun stuff." It made the woman laugh and Tasha grinned with delight.

The food arrived and her hostess sat facing her. "Sorry. I teach school, elementary school. Anyway, as I was saying, I grew lonely, moved the guy in with me. That's when it started. Rather classic, I guess. First it was dissatisfaction with things I'd do, then harsh words, then a hard shove...that's when I threw him out. I won't put up with that. I shouldn't have to."

"No you shouldn't."

"He came back but I wouldn't let him in. I called the police. They ran him off and I got a restraining order. That just made him angrier. I keep calling the police, but they're starting to take his side, like this is all my fault and I should just shut up and please my man." She sighed and took a sip from her coffee. "I guess it's time to buy a gun."

"Bad idea. Look, don't get me wrong; I'm on your side here, but the gun is a bad idea. That'll just escalate this thing. Let me deal with this guy."

"What can you do about him. I wouldn't want you to get hurt. He's a big boy, and..."

"Look, you saw how that cop reacted when he saw me. He has good reason. Believe me, I can deal with this."

"What will you do?"

Her voice sounded frightened now that the aura of danger had returned to Tasha. Tasha's eyes were hard as she responded. "I'll give him one chance to walk away forever. If he doesn't take it, I'll put him down hard and dispose of the body."

The woman sat back and gazed at her with wide eyes. "You'd kill him?"

"He'll kill you if I don't, sooner or later. You know that's true."

Amelda's shoulders slumped. "I know you're right. I've been so scared. The cops said to run and keep running. That's fine if you have the money to do it and don't mind that kind of a life. Dammit, this isn't my fault. I shouldn't be the one who has to run away. I just don't like the idea of killing anyone."

"And you won't be; that's my job. Look, I know I don't look like much, but I have my ways. My name is Justice, and I will bring justice to you. This isn't your fault, and you won't have to pay the price for it. I have to go now, but someone will be watching the house until I get back."

"Someone will be watching the house?"

"There is a group of war veterans who have formed themselves into a gang. Their aim is to make a safe area for all veterans who are on the streets. This house is within their claimed territory. They were watching this morning. If I hadn't interfered they would have shot the policeman and the landlord. These men are trained killers, and they mean business. This is their territory, the people here are their people, and they will protect them."

"Oh my god. They were watching?"

"Three men. One at the side of your house, one next door, and one in the bushes. They meant business."

"Oh my god," she said again. "How did they know?"

"They make it their business to know what goes on in their territory. This is what they were trained to do, and they do it well."

"How did you know about this?"

"From them. One of them recognized me sleeping in an alley. They came and offered me one chance to deal with it first. They were watching in case I failed. Your house is safe now. I have to go, but I'll be back before nightfall. Thanks for the meal, it was awesome." She rose and headed for the door.

"Hey, no problem, Girl, anytime you're hungry or need a place to crash for the night, you come to me. You hear me, Justice, you come to me."

Tasha stopped at the door and turned. "I'll remember, I promise. You relax now. This will all be over soon." With that she was out the door and gone. The woman hurried to the door to call out again, but the street was empty, no sign of Lady Justice anywhere. She closed the door and locked it.

Tasha jogged for a couple of blocks then noticed some men working at a manhole. One was Decoy. He waved her over then disappeared down the hole. She swiftly followed. The men above moved the cover back into place. A short walk later they were in an open area where Intel and Blockade were waiting. Intel was grinning at her.

"Lady J., you rock. That was awesome. I had that cop in the cross-hairs just waiting for him to go for his gun."

"She was watching him the whole time," said Decoy, grinning. "Lady J. you're amazing. You made that work and nobody got hurt."

"Yet." Tasha sighed and leaned against the wall. "I know how this will go down. I'll tell him to go away, he'll laugh because I'm just a little girl, then he'll get pissed because I'm telling him what to do, threatening him. He'll come at me, I'll take him down, and then it'll be over. The woman won't get hurt and will keep her home, the landlord has the cops off his case and keeps his favorite tenant, and the abuser goes away forever. Justice is served."

"And the fat cop?" asked Blockade.

"I'm hoping he learned something." Tasha checked the floor to make sure it was dry then sank to a cross-legged sitting position. "I don't think he's really a bad guy. I think he was bullied as a kid and joined the police so he could be the bully. Don't get me wrong. If he crosses the line he pays the price. I just think the guy may be worth a second chance."

Intel looked puzzled. "Why, Boss?"

"It was the night I got caught and thrown in jail. Jess did her best to protect me. He shot my cell phone, saying it was no good for evidence. Then he warned Jess that the other cops would try to kill me."

Intel nodded. "You could be right, Boss. I wouldn't trust him too far though."

"I won't. I gave him a fair chance. If he blows it he pays the price same as anybody else."

"So, what's the plan for the rest of this?" asked Decoy. "You know it isn't over."

"I know. I assume Finder is watching her place."

"He is."

"So she's safe enough for now. I'll go back at dark and wait for the guy to show up. I'll do that as many days as it takes. Right now I need a nap. I get the feeling it could be a long night."

Intel nodded. "I'll take the watch, wake you at sundown." He nodded at the other men and they rose to their feet, saluted then trotted off. He turned his back to Tasha and settled down to watch the entrance to the hidden room.

She didn't immediately fall asleep. Instead she called silently to Moragah. *"I am here, my priestess. You handled that situation today perfectly. I am quite proud of you."*

"Thank you, my Lady Goddess."

"You are concerned. What troubles you?"

"Nothing, and that's the problem. Moragah, I was fully prepared to kill that policeman and I am expecting to have to kill that man whenever he shows up. I feel nothing, nothing at all. No remorse for what I've done or will do, and no fear at all except for the woman he abuses. That scares me a bit. I don't want to become like those guys."

"Do you feel any thrill at what is coming? Is there any joy for you in the killing? Does it give you a sense of power, of delight in your superiority?"

"No. Oh gods, no."

"Then you will not become like them for that is what they feel. That is what motivates them, the bullies and abusers. You are not like them, my Dark Priestess. I will admit I have changed some things in you to make what you do possible. Fear, remorse, conscience, at the wrong time can be fatal.

"I took these from you, Tasha and trust in your powerful sense of justice to carry you through on the right path. Know this, death is not the end of your spirit's journey, just another transition into a different state of being. The men you killed are on that journey now and can do no further harm here. It will be the same for the rest of those you encounter."

"I felt compassion for that cop though."

"Of course. I left that with you, for without it you would not know what is just and what is not."

"Thank you for that. I don't think I would be human without that. That's what's wrong with them, isn't it? The bad guys, they lack compassion, don't they."

"*Yes, that is what allows them to do what they do.*"

"What about my soldiers? Do they lack compassion too?"

"*No, but they have been trained to suppress it. That is why so many of the veterans are so deeply troubled. They cannot reconcile what they have done with what they know to be right. I have eased that for the soldiers closest to you. You will need them in the coming days.*

"*Tasha, I know what is coming for you. I now remove all restrictions from you. You no longer need to provoke those whom you face. I leave it all up to you now and trust in you fully.*"

"You're not leaving me?"

"*No, no, my priestess. Never that. I will always be with you. I only do this to increase your survival chances. There will be a time when you will be hunted and will need to act without restriction. I trust you to do what you must and only what is needed.*"

"Lady Moragah, promise me you will stop me if I get out of hand. Remind me of who and what I am supposed to be."

"*I promise, my priestess. Rest now. Be at peace.*"

TASHA KEPT HER VIGIL outside the woman's house all that night, and the next. It was the third night when the man showed up. An old car stopped in the driveway and a tall man got out. He looked angry and determined. "I know you're in there, Amelda. You better not have that door locked. I'll kick it in, I swear I will."

He took a step forward and reached for the handle. Suddenly a small figure was between him and the door. She thrust her hands against his chest, causing him to stagger back, nearly falling.

"What the fuck is wrong with you, Kid? You got a death wish? Get your stupid ass out of my way before I slap the shit out of you." She didn't respond, nor did she move. He came at her then, reaching to grab her by the shirt front. Tasha ducked under his hands and thrust him back again. This time he did fall. He scrambled to his feet, pulling out a huge hunting knife.

"You can't go in there. I'll give you a chance, only one. Go away and never come back. Do that and we're done; come at me again and you die where you stand."

"You stupid little whore; I'm gonna fuck you up ugly." He leaped at her, thrusting with the knife. Suddenly he wasn't able to catch his breath. Looking down he was surprised to see the knife protruding from his chest.

He barely felt the blow to the back of the knee that started his fall to the ground. Helpless, he watched as she raised her foot and stomped the handle of the knife, driving the blade further into his chest, slicing through heart and lungs.

As his life slipped away a big soldier appeared. He was aware of the man reaching for him then nothing more. The soldier threw the body into the back of the car then turned to Tasha. "I'll just dispose of this garbage for you, Ma'am." He climbed behind the wheel and started the car.

As Blocade drove away, Decoy came around the house with a water hose. He washed away all signs of blood then disappeared around the house again.

Tasha knocked softly on the door. The woman had watched the whole through the window. Tentatively, she opened the door. "You have nothing more to fear from that man, Amelda," said Tasha. "Justice has been served."

"He had a knife. That knife was intended for me, wasn't it?"

"Probably, but it's been dealt with. You're free of him now."

"How can I ever thank you?"

"Live a long and happy life," replied Tasha, "but be careful too." She turned and walked away.

Amelda started to speak again then was shocked to realize Tasha had disappeared. "How the heck does she keep doing that?"

"It's a mystery to me," said Decoy as he reappeared again. "Her name is Lady Justice. You never know where or when she'll pop up. Since we claimed this territory, she said we had the job of cleaning up her mess. I'm happy to report, job done. I'll just be on my way, Ma'am. Lock your doors now." With that he too disappeared.

Amelda withdrew into her house and locked the door tightly. "In the eyes of the law I am now an accessory to murder," she sighed to herself as she poured a tall glass of wine. "Ah, to hell with it. At least now I don't have to lay awake at night waiting for him to kick in the door and beat me to death. Like she said, Justice has been served."

Storm's Coming, Get Ready

T asha arrived back at the hideout, tired and hungry. Intel was there, but his mind seemed to be far away. He gestured at a cooler and she peeked inside then smiled with delight. As she reached for the chocolate milk he hurled a wad of balled up paper at her. She slapped it away without even looking.

Pulling out a sub sandwich to go with the chocolate milk, she turned back to face him, placed her back against the wall and slid down to a sitting position. Folding her legs under her she took a bite of the sandwich and chewed thoughtfully while gazing at him. Finally she spoke. "I can hear your wheels turning. What's up?"

"There's been a lot of quiet interest on the street. Interest in a crazy girl who kills nasty cops. It's really quiet, but it's there. They're hunting for you and they're getting far more serious about it. Sooner or later, somebody will talk. They always do."

She just nodded and continued working on her sandwich, so he continued. "I think it's time you started training, Boss."

"Training? You mean like boot camp? Push-ups and stuff?"

He sighed and gazed at his hands for a moment. "Look, I know you can do push-ups with me on your back and do 'em all day. That's not what I mean. I'm talking about climbing, jumping, dodging. Evading skills, escape skills, avoidance skills."

She drained the last of the chocolate milk and sighed as she set the container aside. "Yeah, I guess that does make sense."

"And then there's the other."

"The other?"

"The other stuff you do, like the hiding in plain sight invisibility thing you do. Can you do it on the move or do you have to be standing still? The long-distance hearing, you have to focus, but could you train yourself to do it automatically? You know, catch something unusual without even trying? You say you instinctively sense danger. Can you hone that skill? These are the things I think you should be training."

"Wow. I see your point. I'll be honest here. I don't even know how I would do any of that. No idea where to start. Help me?"

"Love to, Ma'am."

"You've been working on it, right?"

"Yeah, some."

"So, what else is going on? Come on, talk to me. Don't make me beat it out of you."

He chuckled at that and threw another piece of paper at her. "All right, I'll talk. It seems I've been promoted by the guys."

"Oh?"

"Yeah, and it's all your fault."

She was grinning at him now. "Oh, do tell."

"You changed things, Lady J. You and Moragah, you changed things more than you know. Moragah fixed four of us, somehow that has spread."

"What do you mean, spread?"

"Word got out that this area is safe for vets. A lot of the guys and gals have drifted in, lost, confused, you know, in the same shape we were. Anyway, they've signed on to the idea and it has changed them, most of them are trying to get clean, others are clearing the fog, they're finding ways to train their bodies and minds back to military standards."

"Oh crap."

"Yeah, oh crap is right. Girl, the game has changed. These folks are warriors. That's what they were trained to be, what they became, and then it was taken away from them. They've come here to get back their sense of self, of belonging."

"And they find that in a military type setting?"

"Exactly. They all look to me to lead them and I now have over three dozen men and women under my command. I can't talk to Moragah like you do, so I'm just running with it here. We've sworn to help you and that will always be our prime objective..."

"But now the family's grown?"

"That's one way to put it." He sighed and shook his head. "What have I gotten myself into here?"

"I think you like it."

"Yeah, I kinda do. The thing is, I have an idea that could mean a lot to a lot of people, and I think it works well with your objectives."

"I'm listening."

"This area we've claimed, I want to make it more than just a safe place for vets. I want to make it a safe place for everybody, especially you. The plan is pretty aggressive, and it will meet resistance, heavy resistance, but I believe it can work."

"Keep going."

"I want to chase all the cops and gangs out of here, declare martial law, have the vets enforce it. Make the place safe for everybody."

"Wow. They'll call in the military to drive you out."

"I don't think that'll happen. Most are overseas anyway, but home troops aren't likely to go to war with their own, know what I mean? There's lots of areas in lots of cities where the cops avoid going. This won't be any different except the people who live here will feel safe, not be under siege."

"Wow."

"I just need your permission to move forward with the mission."

"My permission?"

"Look, it all comes back to Moragah. If she says it's a go then we move on it. If she says no, then we abort the mission. We swore a bargain with her, to help and defend you and that is top priority, always."

Tasha nodded then closed her eyes and called. "Lady Moragah?"

"*I am here, my priestess.*"

"You heard?"

"*I did. He wants to light a candle to hold back the darkness. I approve and wish him well with the endeavor. He's right, it will give you a safe place to retreat to as needed. Help him if you can.*"

"I'll do my best, my lady goddess."

"*I am quite proud of you, Lady Justice.*" There was a feeling of mirth and love in that voice as the goddess withdrew.

Tasha opened her eyes and smiled at Intel. "Okay, I'm in, what do we do first?"

He smiled and sighed with relief as his shoulders relaxed. "First you sleep, then tomorrow we start your training." He rose and left the car so she could have privacy to rest. He threw another ball of paper at her as she glanced away.

Tasha batted it aside easily. She smiled as she heard him pause at the small altar. "Thank you, Moragah. I swear I will always make her safety my first concern, but I do need to make a place for those like me. Thank you for blessing my efforts. For Moragah, for Justice, for freedom."

THE TRAINING WAS HARD, harder than she would have thought possible. She was kept in the hideout or the sewers, always in darkness. People were there, throwing things at her, pointing weapons at her, always without warning. After a week of this training her senses were much sharper, her hearing attuned, and she was enjoying it.

The next week they moved into the streets, back alleys, subway stations with lights. Now people were using paintball guns. After the second day her clothes stayed clean. On the fourth day she seemed to disappear, suddenly reappearing beside or behind her stalkers to slap a butt, pinch a belly, or blow in somebody's ear.

By the end of that week she could stay hidden while at a full run and still follow a conversation that was going on a block away. She could jump over twelve feet in the air and climb a seemingly straight wall. And her strength was increasing.

At the end of the second week she disappeared. After several hours of searching, they gave up and regrouped at the hideout, renamed it headquarters, and began to organize themselves into a functioning military unit. Finder took Blockade and went to gather weapons.

JESSICA GOT HOME AND stepped through the door, kicking off her shoes. Her suddenly alert instincts brought her silently to the kitchen, gun in hand. There was a single rose in a glass of water on the table. The note beside it simply said, "For the cook."

"Well there's a hint if I ever saw one. Bet she's asleep on the bed again. Ah well, cook it is. Now what do I have to feed a hungry crusader?"

She began to hum softly as she worked. Jessica wasn't sure when she first heard the flute playing the song she was humming, but the sound was coming from the bedroom. "You might as well come out here. I'm not bringing you dinner in bed." A silvery laugh replaced the flute then Tasha appeared from the hallway.

"Mmm, Jess, that smells divine."

"Wait'll you taste it. Hungry?"

"Starved."

"Like always. Sit and I'll feed you." She just shook her head as Tasha devoured the plate of food. "When was the last time you had a decent meal?"

"When was I here last?"

"You're serious?"

"Yeah, I pick up a few meals at different soup kitchens and such, but it's a long way from regular and none of them cook half as good as you."

"Oh yeah? You think flattery will get you another plateful, do you?"

Tasha grinned as she held out her empty plate. "Please, Ma'am, can I have some more?"

Jessica chuckled and rose to refill the plate. She set it before Tasha then resumed her seat. "You're just lucky I enjoy cooking."

"Yes I am, and believe me, I know it. Jess, thanks for this. It's awesome. Now, tell me what's up."

"Actually, two things. First, the commissioner is really putting the pressure on the chief to find you. Tasha, I can tell by the way this is shaping up, they're going to put on a major sweep of the ghettos. I assume that's where you've been hanging out."

"Sort of. There's a bunch of military veterans down there who have formed a street gang of sorts. They've claimed a territory for themselves. They're keeping the peace, so I retreat to their territory to sleep. Safer that way."

"Really, so you sleep someplace else besides my bed?"

"Well, you know, if you gave me a key I could..."

"Shut up, Justice, I don't want to hear it. Besides, a key? Since when do you need a key?"

Tasha gave a soft giggle then sobered. "I know they're building up for a major manhunt for me. That's only to be expected. What was the other thing?"

"I hesitate to mention it. I doubt there is anything you can do about it anyway." Tasha just waited patiently for her to go on. "Okay, it was early last night. They brought in a guy, half dead from the beating. Apparently they stopped him for a busted tail light. I saw the video of the arrest. The guy didn't fuss, fight back, try to run or anything.

"Goddam it to hell, this is not police work." Jessica was on her feet pacing, waving her arms in frustration. "There's no excuse for any of this. They just went at the guy because he was black. When I got there this morning there was fresh blood on him. They'd beaten him again in the night." With a sigh she resumed her seat. "I'm not sure if the poor bastard will survive another night."

"You want me to break him out of jail?"

"Can you?"

Tasha thought for a moment then sighed. "Yeah, I think I can. This will be a real test of my training."

"You've been training?"

"Yeah, with the soldiers. Intel says he's turning me into the ultimate infiltrator. I guess we'll see if he's right or not. Can you give me a lift to the station? Just drop me off a block or two away."

"Sure, I can do that. Oh, thanks for not killing Martin. You did scare the crap out of him though. He's lost the attitude and is almost human these days. I owe you for that one. Did you fix the problem for that woman?"

"Justice is served. She'll have no more visits from that guy. So, are we going now or are you going to make me wash the dishes first?"

"Depends, did you make up the bed again?"

"Not a wrinkle in it."

"Then you're clear. Let's go."

Tasha stood outside the police station, hiding in the shadows at the edge of the parking lot. She could hear seven different people inside. She was scared, her hands shaking. "Stop this, Tasha, you have a job to do. This is just another distraction to be dealt with. The main thrust is to get justice for your mom and dad. Maybe we can learn something here about that as well." She drew in a long deep breath then continued her self admonishing pep talk. "You can do this. You've been training. Just do it."

She drew another deep breath as a policeman reached the door and swung it wide. Tasha shifted onto combat mode. The policeman felt a gust of wind, but saw nothing. The door swung closed behind him and he continued on his way. As his cruiser left the parking lot, Tasha stood against a wall, taking stock of the room.

One man was at the front desk, his head down over some paperwork, two more were talking by the coffee station, and two more were facing the holding cell where a man on the floor moaned and begged for help. Tasha moved again.

The man at the desk didn't know a thing as his head was smacked against the surface of the desk. The two at the coffee station had their heads cracked together, both fell to the floor, unconscious, and the final two got rammed against the bars of the cells. The air whooshed from their lungs and they slid towards the floor.

Tasha reappeared, breathing deeply, as she stripped the weapons and keys from the two men. They groaned and tried to grab at her as she unlocked the cell. The man inside was badly battered, and he groaned in pain as she raised him to his feet. "Can you walk?"

He was breathing in short gasping breaths. "I think so. Who...?"

"My name is Justice. Don't try to talk now. We have to get you to a hospital. Are these two the ones who hurt you?" He nodded and pointed at the two trying to regain their feet. "Okay, you lean on this desk for a minute."

She propped him against a desk then grabbed the two men and thrust them inside the cell, locking it behind them. Their weapons were gone and so was one man's wallet. They were shouting vile threats as she helped their victim out of the building.

Outside Tasha used the remote on the keys she'd taken from the two in the cell. An unmarked car beeped and flashed its lights. She tucked her man in the passenger's seat then drove straight to the nearest hospital. As she helped him inside, people came to assist. "This man is a police officer; he's been badly beaten. Here's his wallet with his ID and medical insurance cards inside."

"Miss, you have to sign..." It was a waste of breath, she was already gone.

Tasha drove back to the police station. Listening carefully, she heard nothing but the pathetic bitching of the two in the holding cell. She was back inside in a heartbeat. First she dragged the two men from the coffee station to the cell and put them inside with their buddies, then returned for the last man. A few slaps brought the man at the desk back to consciousness. "Ow, my head. What the hell happened?"

"I smacked you down."

"Oh my god, it's you..."

"Yeah, it's me. You want to keep breathing, do as I say." He just nodded. "Good boy. Now, I want the personal belongings of the man who was in that cell."

"In the evidence room."

"Lead on. Try anything funny and you're finished." He did as she told him, terrified of the teenage cop killer, as they called her. He passed her a large envelope with personal effects. "Good, now back upstairs. I want his file and the file you people have on me."

As they arrived back upstairs there was a frantic voice on the radio trying to get a response. "Ignore that. Get my file, and fast." He hurried to one desk, flipped through a few files then passed first one then another to her. "Thanks. Now you'd better talk to the guy on the radio. He sounds worried."

At that she shifted back onto combat mode and disappeared from the police station. Within a half hour the SWAT team from central was at the station, a hard search went on all night, but she was nowhere to be found.

Jessica Logan sighed again; sleep continued to elude her. A faint sound in the room sent her rolling to the floor then coming up with the lights on and gun in hand. "Freeze right... dammit, Tasha, what the hell are you doing, sneaking through the window in the middle of the night? Are you crazy? Are you trying to get yourself killed?"

"I have to use the window. You won't give me a key."

"Shut up. I should smack you for scaring the crap out of me. So, how did it go? Were you able to? Tell me you didn't kill anybody."

"I got him out, didn't kill anybody, got him to the hospital, used one of the cops insurance to get him admitted then went back for his stuff. I'm hungry, any of that delicious supper left?"

Jessica followed her to the kitchen. "You got his stuff?"

"Yeah, and the file they have on me. Jess, I know I scared those guys tonight. I won't dare try that again, they'll be ready for it. There was hardly anybody there, is that usual?"

"Everybody out on patrol," replied Jessica. She pulled the plate from the microwave and passed it to Tasha. "After tonight's episode you can bet they'll beef up the security big time. We won't dare try anything like that again."

"I know. I'll admit I was scared to death the whole time."

"You scared?"

Tasha sighed and dropped her chin onto her hands, elbows propped on the table. "Most days I'm scared to death, Jess. What happened to my family scares me, what happened to me scares me, and what I can do scares the hell out of me. I'm still learning about what I can do and how to do it. What's even scarier is how much I didn't want to hold back on those guys."

"You're a good person. I know what you've done, but I also know you're a good person. Anybody else with your abilities would have gone on a rampage, but you didn't. However, I warn you, toughen up a bit, girl. They're gonna come at you hard and fast after tonight. Don't hold back; take care of yourself."

"Thanks, I will. I should get going, now."

"You can crash on the couch if you want."

"Love to, but I have another errand tonight. Rain check?"

"Any time. Any time at all."

Tasha smiled and patted her shoulder as she headed for the door. Jessica stopped her as she turned the knob. "You know, I will get you a key if you want one."

"It's more fun to use the window."

"Go away, crazy woman." Jessica was smiling and shaking her head as Tasha disappeared. Outside Tasha didn't wait for a cab. She kicked into combat mode and ran. She caught the cab several blocks away.

Alicia Murdock swore in most unladylike language as she retrieved the offending cell phone from her purse beside the bed. "Hello? Hello?" No response, but the phone rang again. "Crap, wrong phone. Hello? Lady J.?"

"Hi there, coffee buddy, you awake?"

"I am now."

"You alone?"

"Why Tasha, I didn't know..." That brought a howl of laughter over the speaker.

"Cut that out, you tease."

"Who's teasing?"

"You are. Now that you're awake, can you let me in or is your dad home."

"Dad's at work, we have all night."

"Stop it. Open up and let me in." Chuckling, Alicia swept up her robe, pulling it around her shoulders as she hurried to the door. Tasha slipped inside and Alicia hurriedly shut the door and locked it. "All right, all jokes aside, it must be important for you to be here at this hour. What's up?"

Tasha relaxed into a plush chair then tossed a large brown envelope on the coffee table. "The cops picked up a guy for a busted tail light. Beat him up pretty bad and held him without medical attention."

"Oh shit. That's what had Dad so pissed."

"Yeah, well, tonight I went in and brought the guy out. Didn't see your dad anywhere, though. I took the guy to the hospital, the Lady of Grace. I used one of the cop's insurance to get him admitted."

"Now that's justice."

"Thought you'd like it. Anyway, that's the guy's personal belongings. Can you get them back to him?"

"Love to. Can I interview him too?"

"Nope, at least not yet." Alicia gave an exaggerated pout. "Stop it. If you do that they'll make the connection to me. Both you and your dad will get killed. Get his stuff back to him. When it's safe I'll give you an interview."

"You will? That's awesome. That interview could guarantee me a job at the TV station."

"You're serious about this, aren't you?"

"I am. I'm so ready for this."

"In a hurry for the career to start? Can't wait to graduate?"

"It's only a few months away."

"Okay. Look, get it done. Graduate then I'll set you up with interviews that will make you a woman in demand. Just promise you'll be careful."

"Why, Tasha, I didn't know you cared."

Tasha was laughing. "Shut up, Alicia. That's it, I'm going home before the neighbors call your dad and tell him you've got a boyfriend in here."

"He'd never believe it. He knows I like girls. Now, a girlfriend he would believe."

"You're a bad woman and I'm leaving." Tasha went to the door and unlocked it. "Lock up tight behind me, okay?"

"Promise. You be careful, Lady Justice."

"Always."

Tasha slipped through the door and disappeared into the gloom of night. Day was dawning when Intel heard the soft, "For Moragah, for Justice."

"Busy night, Boss?"

"Extremely. I'll tell you all about it after a week of sleep." He chuckled as he closed his eyes again.

While Tasha slept the day away, the police manhunt went into overdrive. No matter who they asked, or what surveillance recordings they looked at, the only place they found traces of her was near and inside their own station.

Meanwhile a man who'd been badly beaten lay quietly watching television. He'd been told his medical covered everything and he had just nodded. They'd called him by the wrong name. He didn't care. They'd helped him. They told him the young woman who'd brought him in saved his life. If he'd waited longer to get medical attention he wouldn't have survived.

He was still mulling it all over in his mind when the nurse appeared in the doorway. "Officer Billings, you have a visitor. I think she's a reporter."

The nurse scooted out, admonishing the visitor to not stay long and overtire him. He watched as another young woman approached. "Charles Dennis?" she asked softly. He nodded. "I'm a friend of a friend."

She slipped a large brown envelope under the blanket of the bed. "This is your personal effects. My friend brought them out of the police station with you. Your police file is in there as well. Mr. Dennis, my friend told them you were a police officer and she used his medical to pay your expenses. I'd advise you to play along for a while until you're feeling better."

Again he nodded. She smiled, patted his shoulder, then turned to go. Feeble, he reached for her hand to stop her. "Miss?"

"Yes?" Alicia took his hand and held it gently.

"Who are you people? I can't tell you how grateful I am. It's all a bit fuzzy, but I think I saw your friend on a wanted poster in the police station. Who is she? Why would she help me?"

Alicia patted his hand and smiled reassuringly. "Yes, she is wanted by the police. Her name is Lady Justice. She was a victim of police brutality too, that's why she helped you. Now, it is extremely important that you don't tell anyone about me, okay? I'm just a junior reporter and you didn't want to answer any questions."

"Got it. I don't know nuthin' about nuthin'. I was too out of it from the beatings. So, you're not really a reporter?"

"Not yet, but I hope to be someday."

"Let me know when you're ready, I'll give you an exclusive." She smiled her thanks. "And thank that friend for me. Lady Justice was it? Tell her I'll pray that they never catch her."

"I will, Sir, I promise."

She patted his hand again then walked away. As she left he opened the envelope. It was all there, his wallet, keys, phone, and the engagement ring he'd bought for his girl. As Alicia strode across the parking lot he was punching in the numbers to call that special girl to let her know what had happened and where he was.

A Hard Search

Tasha awakened with a start. Her instincts were screaming of danger. Intel came running to warn her but she was already gone. "Lady J. if you're still here hiding, get out. Get out now." She watched as he pulled an assault rifle from under a tattered blanket and ran back towards the streets above.

"Moragah, should I be helping them?"

"*They're trained soldiers, Tasha, and they are prepared to deal with this themselves. Your task is greater. Let them protect you this time.*"

"All right, I will. Thank you, Moragah." With that she ran for the door to the railway, but heard voices outside. She turned and fled into the sewers.

Up on the streets she had left behind, things were tense. The police were searching every building and they weren't being gentle as they questioned everyone. What they didn't see at first were the well armed military troops. The police were also heavily armed and well trained. Yes, the SWAT team was there as protection and back-up.

The police were barely halfway down the cordoned off street when an unarmed soldier walked out with his hands spread wide. He was instantly surrounded by drawn guns. "Get down on the ground! Now! Get down on the ground!"

Instead he pointed at one man and that man fell to the ground clutching his wounded shoulder. All police gun were instantly pointing outwards as they searched for the source of that shot. "You men are surrounded," said the soldier. "Lower your weapons. Failure to comply will result in another wound. Fail a second time and we shoot to kill."

"What if I shoot you first, Asshole?" The big policeman was pointing a weapon right at Intel's head.

"Do that and every man on this street will die. My men are well positioned, several are experienced snipers, and they've all seen actual combat. I'll tell you this, they have heavy arms as well, grenades, rocket launchers, and more. This is our territory. We control things here. Put away your weapons and talk to me."

No one moved so he pointed to another man and that man fell, clutching his wounded leg. "Next one's a kill shot," Intel said calmly. He was cold, showing no emotion at all. They began to lower their weapons. "Very good. Now, get the chief of police out here to confer." One man spoke softly into his shoulder mic.

The chief appeared from inside the armored van belonging to the SWAT team. He approached cautiously. "Who the hell are you people?"

"We call ourselves the Soldiers of Justice."

"So you're working for that kid?"

"We work for ourselves and for the people of this area. We keep the peace in this territory, the people come to us if they need justice, and we deliver. We don't want you people here."

"Well that's just too bad, isn't it? We're the police. We go wherever we damn well please."

"You try, you die. I'm not playing here, Chief. We have snipers in optimum placings as well as heavier arms at the ready. We also outnumber you by about three to one."

"I'll call in the real military and blast you out. Maybe even get lucky enough to kill that kid in the process."

"Call for the military, see where that gets you. There's no way in hell they'll start dropping bombs on an American inner city. Also, I doubt you'll be able to find any troops in a hurry to go to war in an urban setting against their brothers, especially guys who have been there before.

"So, tell me why you're so hell bent on killing that girl."

"Why? She's a cop killer, for Christ's sake."

"The way I hear it, your guys gunned down her unarmed parents then tried to kill her too. I've talked to her. She took out the trigger men and now she wants the man who ordered the hit. Somebody ordered that execution, and she will find him. When she does she'll put him down. Like she says, Justice will be served."

"So you admit you're hiding her."

"I admit no such thing. I told you, she's not here. She doesn't live here. Lady Justice is a roamer. She roams around the city taking care of business. Yes, she has been here. And she is welcome to come back, but she's not here right now. This is her city. She could be anywhere."

"Yeah, well we'll just look for ourselves."

Intel started to point to another man, but the chief stopped him. "Wait. Are you fucking crazy? We're the police, for Christ's sake."

"I don't give a shit who you are. This territory is under martial law. We keep the peace here. The gangs already know this, but I'll explain it to you just once, in case you hadn't heard. This is veteran territory. You come in here with weapons, you die. You bring harm here; you don't go back. We take care of our own."

"You're serious. You'd actually kill cops."

"Every fucking one of you. You fire one shot, throw one punch, and no one goes home. Now, if you want to search, go ahead. Be respectful, keep your weapons out of your hands, and we have no problems."

"Sweet Jesus Christ, you really are serious."

"Yes I am. And there's one thing more. You and I are going to wait right here until the search is completed, Chief. You try to walk away and pop goes the weasel. Understand?"

The chief lost all his bravado. He'd been lured out into the open in a street covered by professional snipers. The man who faced him showed no emotion at all. The chief met his eyes and saw only a cold passionless death there. This man would give the order. There was no doubt. He swallowed hard then spoke much more respectfully. "We've got this area completely surrounded. If she's here she can't get out."

"Then go ahead and search. If she's hiding here that will flush her out. Just remember, be respectful, no weapons."

The chief nodded and waved his arm at his men, indicating they should continue the search. "Keep searching. Do as he says, no rough stuff or you'll get us all killed."

"Tell your SWAT team to stand down. They're covered by snipers and their van is targeted by armor piercing weapons." The chief swallowed and did as he was told.

Intel leaned back against a police cruiser as the men resumed their search. He folded his arms across his chest while the chief nervously lit a cigarette. "Tell me chief, why have you got such a hard on for this kid anyway? She's doing you a favor."

"She's doing me a favor? Really? Enlighten me."

"Okay, here's what I've heard on the streets. She took down the guys who murdered her parents. She also busted up a bunch of your bully boys in the station last night. Now, I'll be the first to admit, that was a kick in the ass. That would piss me off too. However, she didn't kill any of those men last night, did she?"

"No. How the hell do you know all this if she's not here?"

"I know because she told me. I was on watch up the block last night when she came by. She told me what she'd done and that you'd likely be strong arming your way through the poorer sections of the city to find her. She headed off down towards the waterfront and I alerted the troops. I had snipers and gunners in position before you even got your pants on this morning."

"Now that I'll believe." The chief sighed and leaned back against the car as well. "Where the hell did you get all the weapons anyway?"

Intel chuckled. "We took most of them from the street gangs that came looking for trouble. They came looking and we gave them what they were looking for. Word went out about what we're doing here and a few vets from other places began showing up, all packing, some heavy.

"You see, Chief, in this country any idiot can possess heavy artillery, and a good many do. Most of them don't have very good security. We've made a few foraging runs into the more upscale neighborhoods. Call it a public service. We're taking the dangerous weapons out of the hands of those who don't treat them with the proper respect." The chief just snorted and shook his head.

"So what's the deal with Lady J anyway? Why the hell did your guys go after her family?"

The chief didn't reply right away. He watched as a group of his men continued to move the search down the street, interviewing people, taking notes, and all the time being watched closely by armed soldiers in ragged uniforms. "Martial law, huh?"

"Yup. You need something from down here, let me know."

"All right, but you didn't hear any of this from me. The Mayor wants to run for congress. He was at that protest rally, spreading the bullshit liberally as usual. The commissioner wants the Mayor's job so he was here too. Something happened, and a bunch of kids taking selfies were in the wrong place. We were ordered to find them and confiscate the phones.

"The guys found out easily enough who they were. All the kids gave up the phones but one. We cleared the other phones, but when the men set out to collect the last one, the commissioner whispered something to my second in command. He spoke to the sergeant and it went all to hell from there.

"Between you and me, she's cleaning out the garbage from the force, but I'm between a rock and a hard place. Look, you've put on a good show here, and I'd be quite happy to leave this area in your hands."

"But the mayor will raise hell?"

"Big time, so will the commissioner. Soldier, I doubt you have a long life expectancy."

"I'm already dead, Chief. Look up my file with the government. It will say, Frederick Eccles, killed in action, and no amount of DNA evidence will change their minds. I'd rather live a short while for something worthwhile than to die in the streets, alone, neglected, and abandoned. They're far too many like me in this country."

"Yeah, and my kid was one of them. He ate a bullet last year when he couldn't access services."

"That sucks. I'm sorry, Chief."

"Thanks. Well, looks like the guys are done. I'll move them over to the next street."

"That's mine too. One on each side of this one. Five blocks by three."

"We're not going to find her are we?"

"I doubt it. From what I hear, maybe you're better off not to find her."

"Yeah well. You know where she is, don't you?"

"Nope. Not the foggiest. It's like I said, Chief. She's welcome here, but this isn't her home. She's claimed the city as her own and she plans to bring justice to it. She said she sleeps in a different part of town every day."

"Yeah, well, it looks like we're done here. What's your name anyway?"

"They call me Intel now. Just ask for me on the street, most folks will know where to find me."

"No phone number?"

"Nope."

"Why not?"

"It's harder to hit a moving target." Intel grinned as he pushed away from the car. "Good luck Chief, and I hope to hell you never find her."

"Yeah, yeah, thanks for nothing." The chief called his men in and moved away.

WHILE THE POLICE SEARCHED the ghettos and poorer areas of the city, Tasha was having coffee at the university with Alicia Murdock. Alicia had loaned her the use of the shower and some nicer clothes. "Alicia, I can't thank you enough for this. It's a bit more girly than I'm used to these days, but it feels so good to get into decent clothes for a change."

"No worries, my friend. I delivered that package like you asked me to. Man sends his thanks plus."

"So he's going to make it? He's going to be okay?"

"As far as I know."

"That's great. Now, tell me what's eating at you?"

"Me? Nothing."

"Liar, liar, pants on fire. Talk to me woman."

Alicia sighed and began to study her hands. "That's it in a nutshell."

"Huh?"

"Not a woman, not really. My prof found out I'm trans. He had a fit, started yelling about Christ, the bible, and the safety of the children. He threw me out of his class. I'm not going to graduate. I'm completely screwed."

"Oh crap. What an asshat."

"Yeah, well, he threw the fit in front of a lot of people. Embarrassed doesn't begin to cover how I felt."

"Dirty son of a ..."

Tasha was interrupted by the mayor's face on the big screen. "The people of this city won't stand for this kind of lawlessness. This woman has declared war on the police of this city, on the very idea of law and order. She will be hunted down, and she will be stopped. If it's war she wants, it's war she'll get.

"Take a hard look at this picture. If any of you see this woman, call this hot line number on your screen. There's a reward for information leading to her capture." The mayor's face disappeared as one of the waiters flicked the channel to a baseball game.

"Well, shit. There goes my afternoon." Tasha sighed and started to rise.

Alicia stopped her. "Sit. Don't be so silly. Listen. That was a mug shot of a girl who'd been hiding on the streets. Now, you've seen our waiter a couple of times. If he walked past you in a tux would you recognize him? No, and nobody in here will recognize you either.

"I've got a brilliant idea. Drink up, we're going back to my place. I've got an plan and I'm a whiz with a sewing machine."

"ALICIA, YOU'RE COMPLETELY nuts, you know that? God I feel silly."

"No, Justice, this will work. Come on, look fierce." This only made Tasha laugh. Actually it was more of a nervous giggle. "Come on, girl, be serious. Think about it. Everybody's looking for a street girl, a hardened killer. Give them what they expect then when you walk by dressed like anybody else, no one will recognize you at all."

"A cape, Alicia? A friggin' cape? Really?"

"It's not a cape, well, not actually. It's a cloak. Think of it as a long coat with a hood. Besides the t-shirt looks great."

"The t-shirt is too tight and you're looking at my boobs, you perv."

"Can't help it, you've got great boobs, and yes, I admit I'm a perv. Yes, you do need a bigger t-shirt. However, you get the idea here. This will work. You know it will. Just look in the mirror. Tell me this won't work."

Tasha took a long look in the mirror. Alicia had put her in darker make-up with bright red lips. She pulled the hood forward to slightly hide her face and glared at the glass. Sinister. That was the only word that came into her mind. She looked sinister. "All right, you got me. How long will it take to get ready?"

"Come by again tomorrow and I'll have it ready. You'll need combat pants and boots to match."

"I'll get those myself. I don't want anyone piecing this together and coming up with your name. Promise me you'll be careful."

"I promise. Now, wear that home and scare the guys. What's his name again, Intel?"

"Yeah, Intel. Want me to set you up?"

Alicia laughed and steered Tasha towards the door. "Get out, crazy woman."

The next day Tasha returned. She carried a backpack and looked like any other teenager in the city. "Lucky I have a young face." She'd caught her reflection in the glass of a window. "I can get away with this disguise for a few years yet." She lightly tapped on the door and was instantly let in.

There was a lot of banter, laughter, and some fussing, but Tasha was finally in costume. The make-up was more sinister now, the t-shirt had a bright blue J on it as did her forehead. Combat boots, military style pants, and the dark cloak finished the outfit.

"Wow, you're scary."

"Shut up, Alicia. Oh heck, I have to admit, you're right. Once a few folks in the media get a load of this no one will ever recognize me on the streets."

"Great. I've got my phone all ready. Let's do that interview you promised."

"What? What are you talking about?"

"You promised me an interview to help me get a job."

"Once you graduate."

"Yes, but that's been put back a year. I can pick up that course from another prof. Next year maybe, but for now, it's off. Come on, Justice. You can't make me wait another year."

"No, I guess I can't. All right, but you'll have to protect me from your dad."

"Deal, now for some subdued lighting." Alicia turned back the lights then looked around critically. A few swift moves and she had the pictures off the wall exposing the holes and scarred paint behind them. "Okay, you stand in front of that wall. Good. Now do your disappearing thing and I'll give you an intro."

Tasha moved against the wall and Alicia almost did a double take. From barely a few feet away she had to strain to see Tasha standing there. "Great. Now, look fierce and I'll start."

Tasha stuck out her tongue and Alicia grinned then started the intro. "This is Alicia Murdock coming to you from an abandoned building in the heart of the inner city. I've been called here to interview the vigilante known as Lady Justice. She said to meet her here, but, geez!" Tasha suddenly stepped in front of the wall as though she had just walked through it. There was a look of tightly controlled rage on her face. Alicia swallowed hard then continued. "Sorry, sorry. Are you Lady Justice?"

"I am."

"Can you tell me a bit about yourself?"

"Don't be stupid. I called for you because I have a message for the mayor of this city." Tasha moved the hood back from her face slightly, growing more sinister as she moved closer to the camera.

"Hear me well, Mr. Mayor. My name is Justice. You've made wild claims about me declaring war against the police. You're dead wrong. A few weeks ago the police killed my unarmed parents. I found and killed those men. Justice has been served. I'm still looking for the man who ordered them killed. When I find him he will face Justice like the others."

Tasha stepped even closer, fairly trembling with the effort to hold herself in check. "Furthermore, Mr. Mayor, you will have your war. In future I will patrol this city. Wherever I find police brutalizing the innocent or the weak, I will intervene as I did a couple of nights ago when I took a badly beaten man out of the downtown holding cells. I will not be gentle. I will not give second chances. I am everywhere,

I'm always watching. Cross the line and pay the price. Justice will be served."

Alicia's jaw dropped as Tasha stepped back and seemed to disappear into the wall. That's when she realized her hands were shaking. Quickly she shut off the phone. "Dear gods, when I said you were scary I had no idea. I'm sure glad you're not on my trail."

"Get that off your phone right now. Put it on a memory stick and give me a copy for safe keeping."

"Yes ma'am, I work as we speak."

Together they watched the interview. It was a bit shaky, but the face and message of Lady Justice was quite clear. "Think that'll do it, Allie?"

"Oh hell, yes. If that doesn't land me a job, nothing will."

"Okay, you go shop that around, see what you can do with it."

"Wait, J. I've got something else for you." She handed Tasha a piece of paper.

"Monisha Kells? Who's she?"

"She's the young woman who was at that rally that night. She's the one who was talking to the mayor and the commissioner."

"Wow, thanks, Allie. That's great work. I'll look her up and see what her story is."

"Are you going to change before you leave this house?"

"What? Oh crap, I've still got the war paint on. It's already dark out, Think I'll leave it on. Later!"

"Later, crazy lady." Alicia sighed as she closed the door, then suddenly danced around the living room, shrieking with delight.

JESSICA FINISHED HER shower and was drying off as she returned to the bedroom. Suddenly her instincts went on full alarm, someone was in the room with her. There, on the bed, a hood pulled up, was a figure. "As usual." She pounced on the bed. "Gotcha!"

Jessica screamed as the ghoulish figure turned in her arms, wild eyed. "Boo!"

"Jesus Christ. Goddamn you, Tasha Stewart, you scared the shit outta me." Jess swept up a pillow and began to beat Tasha with it. "What the hell is the matter with you? Halloween is weeks away."

Tasha was howling with laughter as she tried and failed to escape the beating. "You should have seen your face, Jess."

"Shut up." That command was followed with another blow with a pillow. "Shut the hell up and stop laughing at me."

"Sorry."

"Sorry my ass. You are no such thing. You're way too pleased with yourself. Now I expect you'll want me to cook for you as well. Not gonna happen."

"Aw, Jess. You're the best cook in the whole world. You know you love to cook for me."

"The hell I do. You'd eat me out of house and home if I let you."

"Jess."

"What?"

"You've got a great body."

"What??? Oh shit." Jessica had lost her towel in the skirmish. Tasha was off in another fit of laughter. Jessica swept up the pillow and smacked her again. "Stop it, you perv. Get you ass in the shower and clean that goop off yourself."

"Yes, Ma'am. Jess."

"What?"

"You can watch if you want to."

"Oh you perv. That's it." Jessica swept up the towel and Tasha ran for the bathroom. She shrieked as the towel snapped across her fleeing backside.

"Gotcha! Tasha."

"Yeah?"

"Fresh towels are in the cupboard. Use whatever else you need. Dinner is in thirty."

"You're the best, Jess. I love you."

"You just love my cooking."

Jessica was singing to herself as she put the final touches on the meal. She smiled as a freshly scrubbed Tasha appeared in clean sweats, singing the harmony. "Sit down, hungry woman. It's ready."

"Ohhh, that smells divine."

"Ha. Wait'll you taste it." Jessica served then sat facing Tasha. "So tell me, what's up with the Halloween costume?"

"It was Alicia's idea," replied Tasha as she took a deep breath, inhaling the aroma of a home cooked meal.

"Murdock's kid? The one who's trans?"

"That's her. She wants to be an investigative reporter. She's been doing some digging for me. She said that if I put on the costume, like batman or something, people would look for that and the real me could move around freely."

"Aw geez. You tell that kid to be careful. Murdock's a straight up guy, but if anything ever happened to his kid..."

"Nothing better happen to her or I will be extremely pissed."

"Oh, now, something going on there?"

"Shut up." Jessica grinned and Tasha reddened. "She's a friend, Jess. She got kicked out of class yesterday because the prof found out she's trans. Apparently he made a real scene. The result is she can't graduate until she makes up the course next year. She wants to get a job as a reporter, so I put on the war paint and gave her an interview. She can shop it around and maybe score a job."

"Oh man, this is a real house of cards." Jessica sighed then shook her head and grinned. "So you dressed up like the crow to help this kid get a job?"

"The crow?"

"You know, from the movie?"

"Never heard of it."

"Seriously? Got any plans for the evening?"

"None at all."

"Fine. I have a copy of The Crow here somewhere. After you finish washing the dishes we'll watch a movie."

"That was subtle. Okay, it's only fair that I clean up. You find the movie while I make like kitchen staff." Tasha sang softly as she worked. This mundane task that she had so resisted most of her life suddenly seemed a delight. It was a simple thing, but a small piece of the life she had lost. It made her smile.

Jessica watched her for a moment, admiring the beauty and grace of the young woman. This was not the soft teenager she had arrested a few weeks past. This girl was a hardened athlete, a warrior. Tasha caught her looking and grinned. "Like what you see?"

"Oh yeah," replied Jessica, licking her lips. Tasha laughed and threw soap suds at her.

"Come on, J. I've got the movie ready to go."

"Well, what do you think?" Jessica asked as the movie ended.

"It was a cool movie. I liked it and I have a lot in common with the hero. All the guy wanted was justice. Actually, he wanted his life back, but neither of us can undo what was done."

"I'm sorry, Tash, I didn't mean to..."

"Relax, Jess, I'm okay. I'm just dead tired and enjoying cuddling against your boobs."

"What??? Oh, you perv." Instead of pushing her away Jessica gently hugged her for a moment. "It's okay to relax once in a while, girl. You're dead beat and hiding behind the jokes. That settles it; you're staying right there tonight."

She gave Tasha's shoulders another gentle squeeze then rose. She returned with a blanket and covered Tasha with it. "Get some sleep, super hero." She patted Tasha's shoulder then shut off the TV and the lights. "See you in the morning."

It's Hit the Fan

J essica Logan felt like she's stepped into a hornet's nest when she got to work. Lady Justice had already been gone when she awakened, a sweet note of thanks on the table. All thoughts of that note vanished in the loud shouting voices of the men in the station house.

The Mayor and police commissioner were in the chief's office. "I don't care what the fuck it takes, Chief, I want that kid dead."

"You mean taken into custody and brought to trial?" replied the chief.

The shouting went on, but Jessica's attention was caught by a young woman sitting quietly at a desk. She looked terrified, but determined. It took a moment before Jessica recognized Alicia Murdock. "Everybody into the briefing room," shouted the newly promoted sergeant as he marched briskly through the room to lead the way.

As soon as everyone was seated he began. "Pay attention, people. In case you didn't see it last night, this was on the news." The big screen lit up and Alicia's interview with Lady Justice played out before them. The room was dead quiet when it stopped. The sergeant gave them a minute to let it sink in.

"Holy shit," came a soft voice from the front.

"Second that, came another."

"People, we've got a problem," said the chief as he marched in. "You've seen that clip from last night's news. Well, there's more. For the few who don't yet know, we ran into heavy resistance yesterday during our search. Map." A map appeared on the screen. One area was outlined in red.

"Look closely at that map. Memorize it. That area has been claimed by a group of ex-military. They're highly skilled and heavily armed. They've declared martial law in that area, no gangs, no criminal activity, and no police allowed. Their leader told me clearly. You bring harm to that area; you don't go home. These people are serious.

"So, here's the problem. He also admitted Lady Justice hangs out there from time to time. The point is, if you find yourself on her trail and she goes in there, let her go. Right now the mayor is talking with the governor to see what can be done about the para-military in that part of town. Until we have an answer, we avoid that area.

"Now, the next order of business. We have the junior reporter in custody, the one who interviewed the killer. Oddly enough, she, he, it, seems to be your kid, Officer Murdock. What have you got to say about that?"

"Not a goddam thing, Chief. As far as I knew she was in school. I had no idea at all about this, but I sure as hell intend to find out."

"Very good, Murdock, you will conduct the investigation. I'll be listening. Officer Logan, you will assist Officer Murdock to interrogate his...offspring. The rest of you hit the streets and find that damned killer." With that he turned and strode from the room.

Jessica followed Murdock back to his desk where they found Alicia with two men in expensive suits. They were the lawyers for the TV station and would be representing Miss Murdock. "What the hell for? asked Murdock. "She's not under arrest.

"None the less, we will monitor the interview with Miss Murdock."

"Fine. Whatever. Right this way, Miss Murdock." Alicia flinched at the sarcasm dripping from her father's words. She made no sound as she followed him into the interview room. Alicia sat between the two lawyers with her father and Jessica facing them.

Bill Murdock sat facing his daughter, drumming his fingers on the desk, saying nothing. Alicia waited for him to explode. It was just a matter of time. Suddenly he surged to his feet, knocking his chair over backwards. "What the hell were you thinking?"

Alicia leaped to her feet to face him. "What was I thinking? I was thinking I needed a job, that's what I was thinking. I got kicked out of school for being trans. I want to be a reporter; you've known that for years."

"Oh for fuck sake." He waved his arms in the air and began pacing about the room.

Jessica grinned as she picked up Murdock's chair and slid into it facing Alicia. "Sit." she motioned with her hand and Alicia resumed her seat.

"You don't have to answer any questions, Miss Murdock."

"I know. Thanks for being here." The lawyer smiled and nodded.

"Alicia, when did the name change become legal?" asked Jessica.

"Last summer, actually."

"What is the relevance of this line of questioning, Officer?" asked the second lawyer.

"Absolutely none at all," replied Jessica. "Sorry Alicia, I meant no offense."

"None taken."

"Will you answer a few questions for me?"

"Depends on the question."

"Fair enough. How did you meet Lady Justice and how did you talk her into the interview?"

"Right place, right time, I guess. I was at city hall, doing research for a paper I'll never get to write now. I was feeling sorry for myself, not watching where I was going. I bumped into someone on the steps. One glance and I recognized her. There were a lot of people around, so I pretended I'd been waiting for her and dragged her off to the coffee shop.

"She thanked me for not making a fuss and I told her I wanted the interview and why. She'd been on her way to confront the mayor and decided this would be better, so she consented. We set it up and the rest you know. I have no way at all to contact her and I have no idea where she went from there."

"Could you take us to that building?"

"Nope. I was met by a soldier who blindfolded me and took me to her."

"What was the soldier's name?"

"Sorry. No can do."

"Fair enough, Alicia. Thank you for being so forthcoming."

"She told me to, Officer. She didn't want me to get into any trouble."

"Well she sure as hell missed the mark on that one." Bill Murdock sighed as he sank into the other chair. "Al, what the hell were you thinking?"

"My name is Alicia, Dad. As I said, I was thinking I needed a job."

"Well you sure as hell got your wish. Now you can learn to live with it. Hand over your cell phone."

"They took that when they brought me in. It won't do you any good, there's nothing on it. Don't bother trying to get anything out of my computer either. I put everything on a memory stick and scoured the hard drive clean."

"So, hand over the memory stick."

"Sure." She pulled a memory stick from her pocket and passed it to the lawyer on her right.

He smiled and dropped it into his briefcase. "Hand it over," said Murdock, holding out his hand.

"Has my client been charged with anything?"

"No."

"Then I'll just keep this for now until she asks for it back."

"Al, stop screwing around and give me the damned stick."

"It's Alicia, and we're done here. Charge me or I'm walking out."

"Our client has been more than forthcoming, Officer Murdock. Do you have a charge pending?"

"No."

"Have a nice day," smiled the lawyer as he held the door open for Alicia who marched proudly out of the building. The lawyer offered her a ride home and she gladly accepted it.

WHILE ALICIA WAS BEING interrogated by the police, another woman was being questioned by Lady Justice. Stifling a yawn the young woman made her way towards the coffee maker. The sun was just beginning to rise. She thought she heard a sound behind her, but when she looked there was no one there. She sighed and yawned again as the coffee started to brew.

"Man that smells good."

At the sound of that voice behind her she screamed and snatched up a knife. "Who are you? What do you want? How did you get in here?"

The figure at the kitchen table smiled and swept off the dark cloak, shook out her long dark hair, and sat down. "My name is Justice. I want to talk to you, and I came in through the door. You need better locks. Can I have a mug of that coffee? It smells divine."

"Justice. You're the one, aren't you? The one the police are looking for. The cop killer."

"Yeah, that would be me. About that coffee."

"What? Oh, sure. Just a minute." Not even knowing why, Monisha Kells put the knife down and poured up two mugs of coffee. "Cream and sugar are on the table there," she said as she set a steaming mug at Tasha's elbow. "So, what do you want with me?"

"Mmm, man, that's good. Okay, first, are you Monisha Kells?"

"Yes, that's my name. What..."

"Relax, I'm not here to cause any trouble. I need your help."

"My help? I don't understand."

"A few weeks ago there was a protest rally across town. We were both there. I was with friends, singing, yelling slogans, taking selfies...stuff like that. Later that night the cops busted into our house, shot Mom and Dad and tried to get me too. They wanted my cell phone. I have no idea why.

"Now, the other day I bumped into a reporter."

"The woman who interviewed you on TV?"

"Yeah, her. She was coming out of city hall. She wanted to know what you and I were doing at that rally. That was the first time I ever heard your name. So, here's what I think happened. My friends and I were taking pictures for Facebook and I think we got a shot of you and some important people who don't want to be associated with you. I want to know why."

Monisha sat gazing at her hands for a long moment. "Yeah, okay. I guess it doesn't matter anymore. I really would like to confide in someone." She paused and took a long sip of her coffee. "I really shouldn't talk to you because I think you're going to possibly kill my father."

"Oh? Why would I do that?"

"Because you've declared war on the mayor. He may be my father, or he may not. It could be the commissioner. Ah, screw it. I'll talk.

"Last year my mother died of cancer. While I was going through her things I found her old diaries. She was in college at the same time as the current mayor and his best buddy, the man who is commissioner of police. Mom had a real crush on the mayor. She went to a party, got pregnant, then had to leave school.

"From what I could gather from the diaries I thought it was the mayor who got her pregnant. I went to that rally to try to talk to him. I'd tried to get an appointment at his office but failed. I couldn't get close enough to him and the commissioner got rough as he chased me away. You guys must have gotten pictures of some of that scuffle."

Tasha nodded her head thoughtfully. "Could be it, all right. There's more to this, isn't there. You said you thought it was the mayor. Not so sure now?"

"No. After that day I came home and thought about it all. The mayor and the commissioner both looked like they'd seen a ghost when they looked at me. I came home and found more diaries. Stuff she'd written when she was so sick. That's where she revealed all, like a final confession on a death bed.

"Mom wasn't impregnated by love, or even a night of drunken lust. She was raped by the two of them. The mayor's father paid her a small fortune to get lost and have an abortion. She took the money and disappeared into the black community of the inner city. She didn't get the abortion."

"So those two morons took one look at you and thought they'd seen a ghost."

"Yeah. They don't know my name cause it's different from my mom."

"That probably all that's keeping you alive," mused Tasha. "Man, that's great coffee. Is there more?"

"I'll get you a refill." Monisha smiled in spite of herself. "You're probably right about that, Lady Justice. I guess we're both on their hit list. I'm so sorry about what happened to your parents. I guess I was the cause of that and I'm sorry."

"You weren't the cause of it, girl. Somebody with a guilty conscience gave the order. When I find them, they're going down ugly. Right now, I think it might be best for you to disappear until I can get this all straightened out."

"I don't understand. You think they will find me here?"

"I did."

"Oh shit. So you did. How?"

"Like I said, that reporter wanted to know how we're connected. If she could work it out, so can somebody else."

"I guess you're right. What am I going to do?"

"There's a woman who owes me a favor. Here's her address. Go to her and tell her I sent you. You need a place to crash for a few days. She'll understand. Once I put this to bed you can come home and resume your life. Oh, and I need your picture."

"My picture? What do you want that for?"

"I want to show it to those guys before I put them down. I want them to know Justice has come home, both for the past and the present." Monisha nodded then stood still as Tasha took her picture.

Later that afternoon a woman answered her door to find a young woman with an overnight bag standing on her stoop. "Yes?"

"Are you Amelda Bradley?"

"Yes. Who are you and what do you want?"

"My name is Monisha Kells. Lady Justice said you could give me a place to hide out for a few days."

"Come in here right now, girl. You can stay with me as long as you need to. Did she tell you she saved my life?"

"No, but that's what she doing for me now. There are people after me."

"They won't find you here. Not before she finds them. Come and sit down, I'll get you something to eat."

THE BIG SOLDIER STEPPED in the path of the woman hurrying along the street. "Ma'am, forgive me, but this isn't a good area for a white girl to be alone on the streets at night."

She stopped and looked up at him. "Are you Blockade?"

He gave her a suspicious look then nodded. "I am."

"Lady J sent me. She said to take me to Intel."

"You're that reporter gal. All right, just a minute. He reached for the radio on his shoulder. "Section nine to headquarters."

"Go ahead niner."

"One of Moragah's children has come for a visit. It's the reporter."

"Bring her in. Relief is on the way. Intel out."

"Acknowledged."

"You guys seem pretty well equipped."

"We are, and getting more so every day. Now, no pictures and no more questions until you meet the Colonel." Another soldier appeared from an ally and Blockade led Alicia down to the headquarters blindfolded.

She shook off the blindfold then blinked in the strong light. "Hi, are you Intel?"

"Yep."

"Lady J sent me."

"Yeah, I got her message. Get comfortable, Alicia is it? Make yourself at home because it'll be a while until we get the all-clear."

AN SUV PULLED INTO Bill Murdock's driveway. Five heavily armed and masked men leaped out, kicked in the door and charged inside, spraying bullets ahead of them. He was waiting for them. He stepped out of the hall closet behind them, his gun at the ready. Before he could fire a shot the gun was snatched from his hand. A blurred figure swept through the room, firing the gun as she went. Tasha came down off combat more, the smoking gun in her gloved hand. The five men were dead on the floor. She tossed the now empty gun back to Murdock.

"Go ahead, call it in now. You were home alone when they broke in and started shooting. You fought back and defended yourself."

"And I killed all five men with automatics with just my police special?"

"That's all an experienced cop like you needs in close quarters, right?"

"Right. I'm a real badass."

"Leave the masks on them until witnesses arrive. Officer Murdock, I've sent Alicia to the soldiers downtown. She'll be safe with them until this is over."

"Thanks for that, Kid. Owe you one."

"Call it in now. The neighbors probably already have. I'll disappear." He was stunned as she vanished through the broken door. He took out his phone and called the station. Nobody would believe he'd been alone, but the only wounds they would find would be from his gun.

Next morning Bill Murdock stood in the chief's office, facing the chief, his first lieutenant, and the police commissioner. They weren't happy. It was the commissioner who was doing all the talking. "How, Murdock? How the hell did a useless old burnout like you take down five men, three trained policemen at that?"

Murdock was pissed and he let it show. "Maybe you should be asking yourself what three cops were doing buddied up with a couple of underworld enforcers. What were they doing at my house, wearing masks, and spraying lead all over hell's half acre?"

"Watch your mouth, smart ass. Now answer my question."

"It's all in my report."

"Tell me anyway, in your own words."

"I was expecting trouble after Alicia's television debut. I heard the car and dove to the floor with my gun in hand. They broke in, started shooting, and I fought back. I won."

The commissioner came around the desk to go nose to nose with Murdock. "And didn't get a single scratch, did you. Bullshit, Murdock. You're the fucking snitch. You're the one hiding that cop killer. That's what happened to those men, isn't it? You had that killer in your house, and she took them down. Isn't that right? Well, what have you got to say to that, Mr. Badass Murdock?"

"My report stands. As for your wild accusations, I say prove it. What the hell makes you think I need a teenage girl to help me against a bunch of your half witted goons. Most of the men you call policemen can hardly tie their own shoes. They're fat, sloppy, arrogant, and useless.

"And, while we're accusing people here, it was you, wasn't it? You're the one who ordered the hit on that kid's family. How'd that work out for you, Commissioner?"

"That's it, Mister, you're suspended without pay. Better yet, you're fired."

"Without just cause? We'll see what the union has to say about that. I'll file suit for wrongful dismissal..."

"Now wait," interrupted the chief, "Just wait a minute, both of you. Murdock, shut the hell up for a minute. Commissioner, he's right. You have no cause. The union will eat you alive on this one. I'll put Murdock on administrative leave until we have this case cleared up. That'll keep him out of sight and if he is the link to Lady Justice that will put a stop to it."

The commissioner didn't like it, but he agreed. Murdock dropped his badge and empty gun belt on the desk. "This is a mistake chief. I'm probably the last honest cop you've got on staff here."

The commissioner snorted. "Get out, Murdock. Hey, where's you gun?"

"Probably in the evidence locker. I didn't have time to check out a new one." With that he turned and walked out the door.

Jessica Logan watched him go then took another step towards the chief's office. She paused outside the door and listened. The chief was speaking. "That wasn't smart, Commissioner, accusing Murdock of being a snitch for Lady Justice. That one will come back to bite you on the ass. He was right though, wasn't he? You did order the hit on that kid's family. Why?"

"Fuck you."

"Yeah, right. Well, Murdock can retire in a few months and I won't be far behind him. Then you can promote this moron here to my job and I won't give a shit what happens to any of you."

"Just keep your mouth shut if you want to live long enough to collect that pension..." The commissioner got no further as a soft knock came to the door.

The chief turned and called out. "Enter." Jessica stepped through. "What is it, Logan?"

"The reports on last night's shooting incident, Chief. You said you wanted them ASAP." She handed him the files and left, closing the door behind her. As she sat to her desk, she sent a quick text. "Come for dinner tonight."

Busy Night

Tasha strode easily along the path through the sewers, her mind wandering. Suddenly she stopped, all her instincts on full alert. She was not alone. A step to the side brought her to the wall and she faded into it. It did no good. A soft haunting voice seemed to come from the sludgy waters flowing slowly by. "I see you."

"Who are you?" she asked. No response. "Okay, what are you?"

A long silence followed, and then the voice again. "Not... not...know. Not you. Go away." Something rippled the waters and Tasha went onto combat mode and fled. In minutes she was far away and climbing up to exit the sewer trail through an open manhole.

She made her way into an alley, and then, as she changed into her costume, she called Moragah.

"*I am here, Tasha.*"

"Moragah, what was that down in the sewer?"

"*Something that should not be, Tasha. Avoid it. Move past that area silently and swiftly. Warn the Soldiers of Justice.*"

"What is that thing, Moragah?"

"*I am uncertain, Tasha. I touched it's essence and it was vile. I have never encountered such a thing before. I will investigate it so we will know how best to deal with it should the need arise. For now, avoid it.*"

"Happily, Lady Moragah. It gave me the creeps."

"*And me as well, not a sensation I am accustomed to. Be wary now, my priestess. You have a busy night ahead of you.*"

"Yes, Ma'am," sighed Tasha as her enhanced hearing detected trouble on the next block.

The big red-faced policeman was bellowing at a woman in a car they had stopped. Tasha could hear the frightened woman's protests and the screams of her terrified children. "I said get out of the fucking car." He reached in and grabbed her by the hair then dragged her through the open window. He threw her face down on the pavement then kicked her.

Several passersby tried to intervene. "Hey, what the hell are you doing? She didn't do anything." That man's cell phone was smashed from his hand as the second policeman began to wield his baton with great vigor. "Stop resisting, stop resisting," he bellowed as he laid about with the night stick.

Suddenly there was a scream of terror behind him and he spun around. His partner was hovering and flailing about above the woman on the ground. It looked like some kind of vampire holding him up. Suddenly she smashed him face first into the pavement, killing him instantly. The cop dropped his night stick and reached for his gun.

The gun was ripped from his hand by the nightmare. She lashed out with a boot and his leg snapped like a dry twig. She tucked the gun into her waist band and looked at him. He whimpered in fear and tried to crawl away. She grabbed him by the broken leg and dragged him back, screaming in pain.

"Stay put. Now, your partner is dead because he abused a helpless woman. I broke your leg because you hit these people for no reason. They were just trying to help her. "Are we done here, or do you want some more?"

"No, no, please..."

"Fine, then justice is served." She turned to the crowd of onlookers. "Don't just stand there recording. Use those damn phones to call for an ambulance for that woman. Do it, now."

"Yes, Ma'am," stammered one teenager.

"Should we get an ambulance for him too?" asked another.

"Suit yourself," she replied then shifted onto combat mode and vanished from their sight.

Tasha was barely three blocks away when she heard a number of angry voices and a scream of pain. She was back on combat mode instantly. She found a group of black teenagers swearing and kicking at a body on the ground. She tore into them like a hurricane. Bodies went flying in all directions, slamming into brick walls, lamp poles, and parked cars. "What the hell is the matter with you people?" she demanded as she came down off combat mode.

"Holy shit, you're Lady Justice," exclaimed one boy as he picked himself up off the sidewalk.

"Yes I am, now answer my question."

"That white bitch got no business in our neighborhood," replied a different boy as he too regained his feet.

"Dear god, you people are so stupid. It's shit like this that keeps the cops mean. This is not the way to settle anything."

"She got no bus..."

"You've got no business." Tasha was angry and let it show. "This is my city, my city. Do you hear me? And this shit has no place in my city. If I ever catch any of you doing something like this again, I'll kill the lot of you. Now, bugger off before I lose my temper."

"Yeah, all you white bitches stick together," muttered one boy as he started away.

Tasha was on him in a heartbeat. She spun him around and threw him against a wall. "Look at my face, Asshole, look at it. Do I look white to you? Do I? I could take that switchblade from your pocket and skin you and that white girl out. You know what I'd see? The same damn thing, that's what I'd see. We're all the same, moron. From now on, in my city, we're all the same. Remember that."

She turned away from him then and helped the victim to her feet. "You okay? Can you walk?"

"Yeah, yeah, I'll be fine. Just bruised a bit."

"What the heck are you doing here anyway?"

"I just moved in. I lost my job and couldn't afford the rent where I was. This is the best I could afford."

"Aw crap. Look girl, you got lucky tonight, but it will happen again. There's a lot of anger and resentment in this part of town. I'm gonna send you someplace safe."

"But, I can't pay..."

"I'm sending you into the Military Quarter. You'll be safe there. You can work something out with the soldiers."

"Hey, look, I'm not..."

"I wasn't suggesting you pay them with sex. Geez, woman. They'll find a way for you to contribute to the greater good and they'll find you a place to stay. You'll be safe there. What's your name?"

"Amy."

Tasha hailed a passing taxi. "Go to the soldiers, Amy. Tell them I sent you." She tucked the woman in the back seat, gave the driver the address of the mission, then closed the car door.

Once again Tasha set out but hadn't gone far before she heard the scream. "Oh come on. At this rate I'll never get anything to eat." She broke into a run. Half a block later she located the problem. A woman was hanging upside down in a tree, her nightgown caught in a branch and a small cat watching her intently. There were also several people watching, all filming with their cell phones.

Tasha burst onto the scene and hurled two young men in the distraught woman's general direction. "Help her. Help her now. If I see one more damn camera going before she is safely on the ground, heads will roll."

"Oh god, it's Lady Justice." Everybody surged toward the trapped woman in the tree.

"And get the damn cat down for her."

"Yes, Ma'am." But they were already talking to empty space. Tasha was gone.

Jessica heard a soft rustle from down the hall. "I thought you were going to stand me up."

"Are you kidding? Miss a meal of your cooking? Hell no."

"You've still got your war paint on. Want to freshen up first?"

"Nope. I'm half starved."

"Okay, I'll feed you first, then you get yourself into the shower and wash your clothes. You smell like a sewer."

"Yeah, well, you tend to when you live down there, not up here in the sun like all you white folks."

"Hey, what kind of crap is that? When did I..."

"Whoa, Jess, Whoa. Sorry. I didn't mean that the way it sounded. Just a joke. I was joking."

"Didn't sound like a joke, Tash."

"Sorry, honest, Jess. I guess I'm a bit rattled."

"Yeah? Tough day?"

"Yes, and then some."

"Care to share?"

"Why not? I'm sure you've guessed it was me at Bill Murdock's place last night."

"Oh yeah, that had Lady Justice written all over it. Nice job. Did you get Alicia out safely?"

"Yeah. She's downtown with the Soldiers of Justice."

"Is that what they call themselves? I like it. Yeah, she'll be safe enough there. So, what else happened?"

"Well, I was on my way back and managed to stop two different cases of domestic violence. I caught a couple of hours nap then started out again. I broke up a street fight then dropped down to the sewers, checked my phone, and realized I should get moving or I'd be late for my dinner date. I turned around and headed this way. That's when it happened."

"What?" What happened? Hey girl, you look a bit freaked out. Tell me what happened."

"There's something down in the sewers, Jess. Something not human, but it can talk. I'll admit it scared the crap out of me. Worse yet, Moragah didn't know what it is either. It creeped her out too."

"Wait, something down there creeped out your goddess? What could do that?"

"I have no idea, but it sure as hell was creepy. Anyway, Moragah is looking into it. Not my job. So, I was on the way over here and..."

Jessica sat shaking her head as Tasha related her adventures. "The whole world going all to pot." She sighed and rose to refill Tasha's plate.

"Thanks, Jess. So, what's up. I got the idea you might have something for me when I got that text."

"Yeah, I do. I overheard something this morning at work. First, Bill Murdock got put off on administrative leave. Basically, leave with full pay, until his case can be closed. The commissioner wanted to fire him outright. They accused him of being your contact on the force. He accused them of putting the hit out on your family. That made them nervous for some reason.

"Anyway, the chief seems to be an honest cop, but the lieutenant and commissioner are thick as thieves. I don't trust either one of them."

"Well, that ties in with what I know. Listen to this." She related her visit to Monisha."

"The dirty bastards. So, now what?"

"Now I keep digging. Here's something that doesn't make sense."

"What's that?"

"Whoever it was wanted my folks dead. I'm starting to think the cell phone thing was just a handy excuse. I think I need to go back to the old house and do some exploring."

"Anything and everything will be in the evidence locker at the station, girl. They really cleaned that place out looking for something."

"Yeah, but they're still nervous. That tells me they didn't find it. I think I'll go take a look; I might get lucky."

Okay, good idea, but not yet."

"Why not?"

"Because all those bags under your eyes aren't from the war paint. Get yourself cleaned up then crawl into the bed. You're dead tired, Tasha. Overtired people make mistakes."

Tasha nodded her acquiescence, she was tired, and that delicious meal was making her sleepy. "Hey, you didn't drug me, did you?"

"Turkey meat, lots of L-Tryptophane, makes you sleepy. Come on now, into the shower with you."

Tasha nodded and headed for the bathroom. Damn that shower felt good. She stayed under the hot water as long as she dared then wrapped herself in a towel and made for the bedroom. Sweeping the towel up wound her long dark hair she fell onto the bed and was soon asleep. She was barely aware as a blanket was tucked around her. "Listen sexy, you're too tired so quit teasing."

Tasha gave a soft giggle. "Rain check."

"Go to sleep, Miss Mischief." Jessica gazed at her for a long moment then turned out the light. She went back to the bathroom and put Tasha's clothes in the washing machine.

Tasha awoke several hours later and found her freshly laundered clothes on the bed beside her. The sky was just beginning to lighten so she dressed in the leggings and an over sized T-shirt she always carried with her. The cloak and combat pants went into the backpack. Once dressed she peeked into the living room and saw Jessica asleep on the couch.

Smiling warmly, Tasha gently lifted the sleeping woman and carried her to the bed. She tucked her in, wrote a note to leave beside her, and then left through the window. Jessica awakened later to find herself in bed with a note. "Hey, sexy, thanks for a great night. I'll call ya, Babe. T."

"Brat," chuckled Jessica as she rose and padded to the bathroom.

While Jessica got ready for her day, Tasha was already at her old home. The place was a disaster. All the carpets had been torn up, the trim pulled off the walls the lights smashed, and the furniture split open and destroyed. "Yep, they were looking for something besides my cell phone all right."

She went to her parents' room. It was the same. The clothing from the closet was all ripped up, the walls torn open, the wall safe open and papers scattered everywhere. Her mother's precious things and jewelry were scattered everywhere. Tasha found the locket with her own and her dad's picture in it.

She slipped the chain over her head then went back downstairs and out to the garage. It was the same there, everything smashed apart, destroyed. She gazed at the old radial arm saw her father had loved. It was broken and he never used it but wouldn't part with it either. Tasha gazed at it thoughtfully. "Why was that?" she wondered.

She began to inspect the old saw closely, allowing her fingers to explore and probe gently. A screw fell out of the cowling covering the motor. It rattled loosely, she gave it a twist and it came away in her hand. There, wedged into the motor, was a memory stick. "Well now. How about that? I'll bet Alicia has her laptop with her, and if not Intel has one. I'll just head home and see what Dad was hiding from the world."

She jogged a couple of blocks then caught a taxi to the subway station.

A New Twist

Home base looked like it was on full alert expecting a battle. Everyone breathed a sigh of relief when she appeared. "For Moragah, for Justice."

"That you, Boss?" called Intel without looking up from his maps on the table.

"Yeah, It's me, Intel. Where's Alicia?"

"She's topside doing interviews for the TV station. They're having her do a piece on the Military Quarter, as she put it. That new gal you sent down here is helping her. They seemed to hit it off pretty good."

"That's awesome. So, why so many guns out down here? Are we expecting company?"

"Unknown at this time. What is known, is this. There's something alive further down the line in the sewers. A couple of the guys have seen something, but they don't know what it is. They say it's creepy as hell. Any chance you could check it out?"

"I met it yesterday."

"Oh?"

"Yeah. I felt it, or something. I went on full hide in the wall mode, but it saw me."

"It saw you? This is seriously bad news. What is it?"

"I couldn't tell you. I was standing there, back to the wall, on full hide me mode, and it spoke to me."

"It spoke to you? What did it say?"

"I see you."

"Oh shit. That is not good."

"It gets worse."

"Talk to me, Justice. How can it get worse."

"It creeped Moragah out too and even she didn't know what it was. She said She'd look into it, but I'm worried all the same."

"Well, that makes two of us. Shit." He turned towards the door and called out. "Mercer, find Decoy, Blockade, and Finder. Bring them here on the double." He stepped to the door as a man hurried up the trail towards the street. "Hear me people. We're on amber alert. Our territory has been compromised, infiltrated. The nature of the intruder is unknown at this time. Stay sharp."

"I'll see if Moragah has anything while we're waiting for the guys." Tasha sank to a cross legged position against the wall and closed her eyes. "Lady Moragah?"

"*I am here, my priestess.*" That vast presence enveloped her and filled her with a warm sense of well being. "*You are curious about the creature in the sewers.*"

"Yes, Lady. Have you discovered what it is?"

"*Yes, to an extent. Long ago this place was sacred to the people who lived on the land. They laid their dead to rest here. After the arrival of the new comers a plague swept the land. The suffering, dying, and the dead were herded to this place and buried, many still alive. Their spirits have long since moved on, but the fear and anger they felt remained behind, intangible, but real none the less.*

"*Long years passed, the city grew, tunnels were built and sewer pipes laid, invading the space once again. That lost, anguished, anger grew stronger. In time it began to invade and posses the creatures that haunt the sewers. In more recent times, caustic and vile toxins were secretly buried and began to leech into the sewers.*

"*These toxins caused changes in the inhabitants down here and they became more susceptible to the influence of the spirit.*"

"Moragah, it spoke to me."

"Yes, for some of the inhabitants of these sewers were human, but this one is no longer. He remains in the waters for there is where he finds food, comfort. I do not think it is a danger to you at this time, but I cannot be certain yet. I will study it more. Tell your people to avoid that place if they can, and if they can't, do not linger there."

"Thank you Lady Moragah. I'll tell the others."

She could hear them returning. There was a chorus of, "For Moragah, for Justice." Tasha opened her eyes to see Alicia beaming delightedly at her.

"Well, you look happy."

"I am, J. I've got a great job, a new helper, and I've got enough interviews to make a great story, maybe even a documentary. I owe you big time."

"Okay, so you can start the payback right now." Tasha rose easily to her feet and tossed the memory stick to Alicia. "See what you can find on that for me."

"Sure. Can I ask where you got it?"

"From my dad's workshop. The cops tore the old house apart looking for something. I'm betting that stick was it. Got your laptop with you?"

"Well yeah, when have you ever seen me without it?"

Tasha chuckled at that. "Cool. See what you can do with that while I talk to the guys here. We have a small problem that needs our attention."

"We're on it, Boss." Tasha grinned as Alicia sat on the floor and Amy sat beside her. Alicia opened the laptop and they set to work.

Tasha stepped to where Intel and the others were waiting. She told them what Moragah had relayed to her. Intel sighed as she finished her story. "This isn't good. We need that route through the sewers. All right, men, we take Lady J's suggestion to heart. We avoid that space, but we need to find a way around it." They set out together to find that new route.

Getting Closer

"**F**or Moragah, for Justice!" They trooped back into the headquarters and flopped down wherever they could find a spot.

"Well, it's a route, but it's a long way from ideal," said Intel as he laid his head back against the wall.

Decoy nodded in agreement. "We can defend against incursion from that direction easily enough, but there's no way to move troops through it at speed. Ideally I'd like to clear the original route."

Finder sighed before he spoke. "Ideally, yes, but we've been poking around down there too much and now we've awakened something that should have remained asleep."

"Yes we did," agreed Intel. "For now we just set up defenses against incursion from that direction. We'll stay well back of the bogey's place for now."

While the soldiers planned strategy, Tasha turned to Alicia who was busy at her keyboard. "Alicia, what's the good word? You find anything interesting on that memory stick?"

"Yep, got the password on the second try then set to work sorting it all out."

"You got the password that easy? Really? My dad was a pretty smart guy. What was it?"

"Every dad loves his little girl. Since it wasn't Tasha it had to be Whitney."

"All right, you rat, how did you find out my middle name?"

"I saw your police file, remember? Don't worry, your secret is safe with me."

"It better be, Missy. So what did you find out?"

"Lots of stuff. I'm trying to put it all in proper order now. Give me a couple of hours to sort it all out."

"Fine. I'll grab a nap and you can wake me when you're ready."

"Will do, Boss." Alicia hadn't raised her eyes from the keyboard. Tasha winked at Amy then settled down on a cardboard bed. She was instantly asleep.

Alicia woke her three hours later. "Tasha, I've got something big here."

Tasha yawned and sat up. "Talk to me, girl. What was Dad up to?"

Alicia sat beside her, sharing the laptop. "It seems your dad was a whistle blower, or he was planning to be. He was an inspector for the city, right? Well, this is a list of inspections he did on his own time. These are all sites owned by a single company. All are in serious violation of environmental protection laws.

"The original inspections were faked and signed off on by the mayor. Now, here's the good bit. The mayor and the police commissioner are major shareholders in this company. They've been dumping toxic waste inside city limits and covering it up. This story could be the making of my career."

"Easy, girl. If you go after the mayor and commissioner you'd better have solid proof. Lots of it."

"I have it. It's all right here. Not just your dad's inspections, but photos, copies of official docs, the fake inspections, the whole works. I've got it all. Your dad's last entry said all he needed was a reporter he could trust with it. Tasha, can I have this? I won't if you say no. This was your dad's work, after all. I'll bet this is why he was killed. They must have caught on to him somehow."

"Dad wanted a reporter he could trust. That's you, girl. Call your own dad and get him down here before you go public with this. They'll go after him the minute you do. They'll threaten his life to shut you up."

Alicia swallowed hard then whipped out her phone. "Dad? Listen to me..."

Tasha rose easily to her feet and approached the table with all the papers spread out on it. Intel was leaning over it, muttering. "So, what's all this?"

"Hey, Boss. We're mapping all the underground routes in our territory."

"Good plan. We need to know every nook and cranny."

"Agreed, but there's a problem."

"Oh? You mean that blank area where the monster lives."

"Yep, that would be it. We're vulnerable there if we don't know the terrain."

"I agree. Want me to scout it out?"

"I hesitate to ask, but..."

"Can it wait another day? I want to pay a visit to the chief of police tonight."

"That would be great. You want company tonight? I've met the chief of police before."

"Thanks, Intel, but I think it will be easier to relax him if I'm alone. I need you here protecting these folks."

"Alicia's father coming in?"

"I sure hope so. He vulnerable where he is."

"I heard that. You got the chief's address?"

"I do and I'd better get going. It's a long hike from here."

The day was getting late when the chief of police arrived home. His wife hurried to meet him at the door. "Carl, There you are. I was just beginning to worry. Hard day?"

"Brutal day, Marsha my love. Brutal day," he replied as he kicked off his shoes, tossed his coat in the general direction of the closet, and followed her to the living room. "The mayor was all over me today. This Lady Justice kid sure has him and the commissioner spooked."

"Well, she is a cop killer after all. I think you should be more worried too. I'll rest a lot easier when she's off the streets permanently."

"Yeah, well, that's not going to happen any time soon. She's holed up with that bunch of crazy war vets downtown."

"No she isn't," came a soft voice behind him.

The chief spun around, gun in hand. The gun was stripped away and he was launched through the air to land heavily on the couch. His wife got off a shot before she too was disarmed and deposited on the couch beside her husband. "Stop with the damn guns already." Tasha came back into sight, breathing deeply.

"I activated the alarm. The police will be here in a moment," said Marsha.

"No they won't. First off, you didn't activate any alarm. Second, they'd stop for coffee and doughnuts on the way to this house."

"She's right there," sighed the chief. He sat up a little straighter. "Look, kid, kill me if you want to, I can't stop you, but don't hurt Marsha. She's not involved in any of this."

Tasha sat in the big chair facing them. "Relax chief. If I wanted you dead it would have already happened. I just came to talk."

"Okay, so what's on your mind?"

"First, I know why the mayor had my parents killed and why the commissioner is trying to get rid of you. I'll soon make them pay for their crimes, but I want the whole story before I strike."

"You mean kill them," said Marsha.

"I do, yes. That's exactly what I mean."

"You call that justice?"

"Yes, Ma'am, I do. Look, you both know most of the police force is corrupt. Put them in jail and they'll either escape or the lawyers will get them in front of a corrupt judge, and they'll walk free. I can promise you; this will not happen."

The chief sighed again. "Yeah, I can't deny any of that, Kid. It wasn't always that way. This force used to be one of the best in the country."

"I believe you chief. That's why I'm here. I want to help you put things back together the way they used to be. I want to help you clean up the police force in this city."

"By killing off every policeman on the force?" asked Marsha.

The sneer in the woman's voice annoyed Tasha. "Lady, you're starting to irritate me. That's a seriously bad idea."

The chief took his wife by the hand. "Marsha, just shut up and listen to what she has to say. Stop needling her or you'll get us both killed. You call yourself Lady Justice, right? So tell me, why is the mayor so hot to see you dead?"

"It's like this, Chief. The mayor and commissioner are involved with a company that is illegally dumping toxic waste within the city. They've taken pains to change the nature of the police force to protect those activities. My dad had proof and was going to blow the whistle; that's why he was killed.

"I've got more on them. When the mayor and commissioner were in college they raped a black woman. She got pregnant and they paid her off to get an abortion. She took the money and ran. Her daughter showed up at that protest rally where I was taking pictures. The cell phone thing was a handy excuse to break into our house and kill my folks."

The chief leaned forward, resting his elbows on his knees. "You've got proof of this?"

"Loads of it."

"Care to share?"

"I gave it to Alicia Murdock. She'll break the story, but I'm sure she'll be happy to share with you."

"Murdock, so he is your contact on the force."

"Nope. I went to his house to kill him, but he had proof of his innocence. I asked him to help me, and he said no. He'd keep his mouth shut, but that's it. He blew a fit when I agreed to give Alicia an interview."

"So why are you really here?" asked Marsha.

"I want to help the chief rebuild the police force into what it once was. I don't enjoy killing, but as long as the police keep brutalizing the population I'll keep putting a stop to it."

"Even if you succeed the police will keep hunting you. You know that."

"I know, but this isn't about me. It's about the people of this city. An honest and respectful police force will have nothing to fear from me. It's about fair and respectful treatment for everybody, black, white, and everybody else in between. It always has been."

Marsha relaxed at last. "I believe you. So you're an idealist. Fine, but you're going to get Carl killed, you know that."

"No I'm not," replied Tasha. "I need him alive. I wanted to give you a heads up, Chief. Alicia Murdock will break the story; the federal prosecutors will be all over you to make the arrests. No way this comes back to haunt you. By the time you show up with the cuffs, the whole city will be in the know. Killing you would be pointless then. The whole thing will be out of your hands.

"The governor will be on your case then to clean up your department and the city. You'll just be the beleaguered chief of police, trying to do his job. At that point, Bill Murdock will be a real asset to you. He knows who's on the take and who's straight up. I'll help."

"Help? How can you help? You're not going to..."

"No Chief, I'm not going on a killing spree. But I can scare the crap out of a few people and your people can listen in."

Marsha shook her head and spoke softly. "Lady Justice, you're not at all what I expected."

"Sorry to disappoint."

"I'm not disappointed; I'm relieved you don't kill without reason."

"No, I don't, but I do kill. The system is so messed up sometimes it's the only way to see any justice done at all. So, Chief, are you in? Do you want to clean up your department?"

"Yes I do, Kid. Okay, I'm in. What's the next move?"

"You keep your head down and watch your back. This will blow wide open in a day or two. Once it does, call Murdock back to work and do your thing."

"There's a slight problem. My Lieutenant is in the mayor's pocket up to his ears."

"I'll deal with him. If I get any more information I'll get it to you through Alicia and her father."

"So, who is your contact on the force?"

"What makes you think I have one? I heard the sergeant confess to giving the shoot order at my house. I put him down. Later I stumbled on a cop terrorizing a woman and her kids. I told him to back off, he pulled a gun and down he went. I learned later that he was the trigger man. Everyone else I just stumbled on by accident. Believe me, if I had an informant there would be a lot more.

"So, we're good here? We have a plan?" The chief nodded. "Okay, then I'll just be on my way." She walked through the door then vanished.

Facing the Unknown

Tasha returned to the hideout by the subway route. It was a quiet night and she arrived without incident. Bill Murdock was there, chatting with the guys. "Hey, Boss. Everything go okay?"

"Yup, all good, Intel. Where's Alicia?"

"She went back to the TV station. Blockade rode shotgun for her. They're all excited about the mayor story and want to run it tonight."

"Awesome. Did she leave us a copy of the evidence?"

"Right here, Kid," said Bill Murdock as he handed her two memory sticks. "She said you'd know what to do with them."

Tasha just grinned. "That's one for us to put in safe keeping and one for you to give the chief of police." She passed one stick to Intel who tossed it to Finder. He dropped it in his pocket. She passed the other one back to Murdock.

"The chief?"

"You'll be getting a call back to work soon," replied Tasha, grinning. "The District Attorney's office will grab Alicia's copy, but the chief will want one."

Murdock grinned and dropped the memory stick back into his pocket. "Kid, you're amazing. I'm starting to believe in justice again."

"Now you're scaring me, Bill." Tasha patted his arm then stepped over to a pile of bedding and settled down.

She awoke to a lot of hustle and bustle in headquarters. How could that be? She had always been such a private person. When did she become comfortable sleeping with people coming and going through the room? "*Your instincts know you're safe, Tasha my priestess,*" came the voice of Moragah. "*You would awaken if danger were near.*"

"I guess you're right. Thank you, Great Lady, for watching over my rest. May your name be blessed this day."

"Thank you, Tasha. Do you plan to confront the beast today?"

"Yep. Today is the day."

"*Be very careful, my priestess. The creature grows stronger and more angry each passing day. It has begun absorbing energy and knowledge from whatever it kills. It's mind is tormented, wracked with pain and madness.*"

"Good to know, Lady. I'll be careful." She swept up her tin whistle and headed out.

"Going exploring?" asked Intel.

"Yep."

"Want back up?"

"That'll just make the beast nervous, but thanks anyway." As she walked away Intel made a hand signal. Several heavily armed men fell in beside him. They followed her at a respectful distance.

Tasha neared the place where she'd encountered the entity. She took out her flute then reached out with her senses. It was there, in the waters, same as before. She began to play, softly, a haunting melody. It was instantly aware of her. "I see you."

She stopped playing. "I know."

Silence followed, then a shifting of a great bulk in the sludgy waters. "More!" Tasha resumed playing.

The beast stilled to listen. She continued to play as she wandered around, making note of the different passages and the directions they ran. As she moved about, softly playing the tin whistle, the beast followed, keeping to the waters. Finally she stopped playing and it became agitated again. "More!" She resumed playing.

Once she had thoroughly explored the area, Tasha decided to experiment. She stopped playing. "More."

"No."

"More!"

"No. What are you?"

"Not know. More."

"No. Where do you come from?"

"Here. Always here. More!"

It was getting seriously agitated. Tasha began to play once again. She played until it was completely at peace once again then stopped. "Are there more like you?"

"No. Yes. Some. Not here. My place. They far away."

"Do you mean there are more like you, but they are far away?"

"Yes. More!"

"No. Can you leave the water?"

"Yes. Sometimes go up to see. Water better. More!"

"No. I have to leave now."

"More!!!"

"No!" Tasha was stunned at the creature's speed as he rose from the water and leaped at her. It was on her before she was fully shifted on to combat mode. It grabbed her with a powerful grip, its clawed and slimy hands burning and tearing at her skin. She broke its grip and kicked it away.

It came at her again, flailing wildly with its enormous hands. "More!"

The thing was so fast Tasha was moving at top speed to avoid it. Slapping its grasping hands away and trying not to hurt it, she ducked and dodged to keep out of its grasp. The beast was getting frustrated. Redoubling its efforts, it managed to get in a lucky blow.

Tasha was sent flying against a concrete wall, the breath whooshing from her lungs. The beast was on her in a heartbeat. Burning hands enclosed her throat and fetid breath steamed in her face. "More!"

Tasha grabbed the thing's wrists to pull the hands away then kicked it solidly in the chest with both feet. The beast staggered back, and she leaped to her feet. Another solid kick to the chest sent it reeling backwards, falling back into the water. Tasha turned and fled. She stopped by her soldiers. "Get back. Come on, hurry. Let's get out of here."

As she herded them away they were followed by a heart broken wail. "More!"

"Boss?"

"Keep going. I don't think it'll follow but keep going. There. That's a good choke point and easy to defend. Take a stand there."

They took a defensive position and waited, but the beast didn't follow. Finally Intel broke the silence. "Boss, what happened?"

"I got my ass kicked, that's what happened."

"Ah-huh."

"Okay. I brought the whistle on a hunch. It liked the music. Every time I stopped playing it wanted more. I made it answer questions then I'd play more."

"Learn anything useful?"

"It's almost childlike. It can speak, think, feel, but I'm not sure about its ability to reason. It doesn't know what it is, but it is self-aware. It's horribly strong, lightning fast, and its touch burns. Lucky I heal quickly.

"Intel, this one is alone. It says there are others, but it didn't know where. Any and all movement through the sewers should be on full alert."

"Agreed. Is it confined to the water?"

"No. It even said it goes topside once in a while but doesn't like it up there." Suddenly they heard the squealing protest of a badly played flute. "Oh great. Now it has my tin whistle. Come on guys, let's go back to headquarters."

"Think it will follow us?"

"No. It'll stay where the water is deep enough for it. It feels safe there."

"Good to know. Did you learn enough to help map out another passage?"

"I believe so. Once we get back I'll draw it out and we can see where the tunnels connect."

She drew out what she'd seen then Intel laid her drawings over what he already had. He soon had a shorter route around the beast. While he worked, Tasha's phone buzzed. "Safe to talk?"

"I'm good, you?"

"I'm at home. Tasha, all hell's broken loose. Alicia broke that story last night. The police arrested the mayor, but he's already out on bail. The commissioner hasn't been charged and he's raising hell. Girl, you've got incoming. They're coming through the sewers. Clear out."

"Thanks, Jess. You be safe. Stay home."

"Can't. I have to go back to work. I'll be riding the front desk while the rest go in after you. Get your people out of there. They're coming in heavy."

"Got it. Later." She shut off the phone. Everyone in headquarters was looking at her.

Tasha just shook her head sadly. "Some guys just don't know when to quit."

"Boss?"

"Intel, it looks like the commissioner has something big on somebody in the District Attorney's office. Alicia broke the story. All hell cut loose, but only the mayor was arrested. The commissioner wasn't charged. Anyway, the mayor's out on bail now and the commissioner has his best troops coming down to take us by surprise. They're coming through the sewers."

"Fuck! Battle stations, battle stations. They're in the sewers. Defense action five. Repeat, defense action five."

Intel continued to shout commands and men scrambled everywhere, swept up weapons, and hurried to their respective positions. "Let me go out there," said Bill Murdock. "Maybe I can talk sense to them."

"Stay back and stay out of sight," said Intel. "You know the rules. You bring harm here; you don't go back."

"Look. I get that, but there's a lot of good men out there who're going to get killed. Innocent men."

"Name one," said Tasha.

"What?"

"Name the good ones. I'll see if I can save any of them, but I won't stop these guys from defending themselves. Name your good cops."

"Well, shit, Jessica Logan for one. That partner of hers for another. He's a bit thick, but he's basically a good cop."

"Logan's on the desk tonight. I don't know about Johnson. Who else?" He didn't answer. "Well, who else?"

"Aw shit, Kid. I don't want this on my conscience."

"It isn't. This is the commissioner's doing. Officer Murdock, you can't wear this one. Those men all know who and what they're facing. They have the option of getting out."

"I guess. I suppose I just defend them because they're cops and it's a habit."

"You're a good man, Officer Murdock. Look, this isn't your fight. You find out about Alicia, is she still free or did they arrest her again? If she's still out of jail, make sure she stays at the TV station, safe. That's your job tonight."

"What are you going to do?"

"I'm going down there to make sure the chief isn't with the incursion group and to get him out alive if he is."

Murdock sighed and nodded. "All right, Kid. Good luck. Stay sharp." He was already talking to her back.

War Beneath the Streets

Tasha started away, but Intel called her back. "Look, Boss, I know you don't like guns, but the gloves are off now. I'd feel a lot better if you'd wear some body armor and carry a weapon."

Tasha gazed at him for a moment then sighed, her shoulders slumping. "All right, Intel. I know you're right. I just don't like the idea of Justice being seen as a warrior, know what I mean?"

"I do, Lady Justice, I do, and I agree with that. However, this is war, so if you don't want to get involved here, I fully understand. Please, either suit up or slip away until the dust settles."

"Dammit, Intel, that was below the belt. All right, what do I need?"

Grinning wickedly, he passed her a Kevlar vest and a helmet. She put them on them he passed her two huge knives and showed her how to put them in her boot so as not to cut herself. Next came the side arm and extra magazines for it and an automatic rifle."

"Won't need the rifle down here," she said. She grumbled as she settled the armor and weapons on her body then set out. As she went deep into the sewers to head off the encroaching police force, she noticed the effect of her passage had on the men. She realized what it meant to them that she would fight beside them. Intel had known this too, that's why he'd bullied her into it.

"*What you do here is just, my priestess. This is truly a battle against the darkness. This must be done.*"

"An all-out war, Moragah? Is this what you wanted?"

"*No, child. This is the last thing I want, but I feared it would happen. If the police get through to your people you know what they will do.*"

"They'll kill everybody then go on a rampage topside."

"*Yes. I applaud your decision to help the chief of police. Therein lies our best hope to hold back the darkness from this city.*"

"Moragah, how many good policemen are in the tunnels right now?"

"*I cannot say. I can say there are several excited at the chance to kill and a few who are terrified. Do what you can, there are no innocents here.*"

"Yes, Ma'am. All right, here we are at the lair of the beast. I'll just slip around without waking him up." Moragah pulled back to let Tasha work.

Tasha slipped around the beast's lair and moved ahead towards the most likely entry point for the attackers. She found the choke point Intel would have preferred to use. He'd held his people back to keep them from having the beast behind them. She could hear the men coming, bitching, and complaining about the smell and refuse. The Lieutenant was leading them.

"Shut the fuck and stop your damned whining. This is our best chance to get that crazy kid and these renegade soldiers at the same time. Every damn one of you will get a medal and your photograph on the wall at the bar, so shut the fuck up. We're trying to surprise them."

"It won't work," said a soft feminine voice from somewhere.

"I said shut up, Kelly."

"I didn't speak, Sir," replied another voice.

"Then who the hell...?"

"My name is Justice. You all know what fate awaits you here. Go back."

"You! Give yourself up. Save a lot of lives tonight. Save your veteran friends."

"Sorry, Lieutenant, no can do. I just came to warn you. You're getting close to the military zone. You know their rules. If you bring harm there, you don't go home. Think about that, people. Do you really want to face hardened warriors in a close quarters battle? They've all been there before. This is what they do best. You're on their home turf. Go back."

"Oh for fuck sake," said the Lieutenant as he opened fire into the passage ahead with an automatic weapon. Tasha sighed and shook her head. She was in a side tunnel, completely safe. However, the gunfire had alerted her soldiers as well as the beast.

"What the hell is the matter with you?" demanded another voice. It was the sergeant commanding the SWAT team. "You've just compromised our mission and given away our position. We should withdraw now while we're still alive."

"The hell we will," snarled the Lieutenant. "This op is my ticket into the chief's job. We push on, clean out this nest of washed up has beens."

"He'll get you all killed," came Tasha's soft voice, floating through the darkness. Several strong lights swept the area and into the adjoining tunnels, but they saw nothing.

"Move out," commanded the Lieutenant. He stepped forward to lead the way. The rest followed.

As they passed her hiding place, Tasha reached out and dragged Martin Johnson away into the darkness. His scream of terror echoed through the sewers, but, hard as they looked, he was not found. Around a corner and behind a broken wall, the policeman trembled in fear. "Hey, Martin, how's it going?"

"You! Geez, you scared the crap out of me."

"Sorry, my bad. Listen, you go any further and you're a dead man. I came to stop you, save your sorry ass."

"Why?"

"Because, in spite of everything, I think you've got the makings of a good policeman. Now, I need your help."

"My help?"

"Yes. Martin, every damn one of those people is about to die. None of them will leave these sewers alive. It's not just the soldiers. There's something else down here. I need you to help me save the good ones."

"The good ones?"

"The straight up cops. Not the bully boys nor the ones on the take, but if there's an honest cop up there I want to keep him alive. Tell me who they are."

"You're serious." Her face told him she was. "All right, you want Kelly and Gomez."

"Just those two?"

"That's where I'd place my bets. I don't know any of the guys on the SWAT team."

"Fair enough, stay here." Tasha vanished from his side.

Just ahead the invaders were about to enter the lair of the beast. "Officer Kelly," came a soft voice from the shadows. Kelly raised her head and that gave her away. She was snatched from the middle of the troop and into the darkness. Her scream ripped through the tunnels, but she could not be found.

Officer Kelly's limp and unconscious body was dropped beside Martin. She was soaked as though she had been dragged through the waters. "She's alive. It was just a sleeper hold. Stay there, I'll bring Gomez if I can."

"Jesus this place is creepy."

"Second that," said another voice.

"Shut up the lot of you."

A soft voice broke the following silence. "Officer Gomez."

"Wha...wha...what?"

That fear-filled response was all Tasha needed. She'd marked her man, but before she could act another voice was heard. "I see you."

"Oh shit," thought Tasha as she edged nearer her man.

"Lieutenant, there's something in the water."

"Probably a lump of shit or something. Keep moving."

"Go away!" The beast rose from the water. "Go away now!"

With that Officer Gomez' scream rent the air as his body was suddenly hauled into the darkness. Bright flashlights lit up the area, but all they found was the beast. The lights hurt its eyes. With a wail of pain, it attacked. Suddenly there was gunfire and screams as the police force tried to fight and flee at the same time.

Howling with pain from gunshot wounds, the beast redoubled his attack. Five of the dozen officers went down to his onslaught, screaming in pain from his blows and the burns from contact with his skin. Those who escaped ran straight into the Soldiers of Justice. They were cut down without mercy.

Officer Martin Johnson sat shivering in the darkness. He was shivering from fear as well as the dampness. Kelly began to stir beside him when Lady Justice reappeared, dropping the body of Gomez beside them.

Kelly groaned and opened her eyes. "What? Where am...oh shit. We're in the sewers."

"Yes you are," replied Tasha as she shook Gomez awake.

"You're that kid; the cop killer."

"Yes I am, but you're still alive. Pay attention and you'll stay that way. Officer Johnson here helped me get the two of you out when it all went to hell."

"What happened?" asked Gomez. "What the hell was that thing?"

"I have no idea," replied Tasha, "but it's dangerous. Listen now, most of your people are already dead. Those who escaped the beast have run into the soldiers. They won't make it out alive. Officer Johnson, take these people and get back to your police station. Report to your chief that you're the only survivors of tonight's incursion."

"Listen, we need to help our brothers..."

"Try that, Gomez, and I will kill you myself. This part of the city is off limits to you. Go back. Stay alive."

"Lady Justice?"

"What is it, Officer Johnson?"

"Which way is out?"

"There, that passage. Take it, and then the first left you find. Use your lights, make sure you don't miss it. That will put you in the main tunnel. Follow that to the right until you find the place where you came in."

"Thanks."

"Don't mention it." With that she vanished into the darkness.

"So, what do we do?"

"We do like she said, Kelly," replied Martin. "She gave us a chance. Let's not blow it."

"But I can still hear the gunfire."

"Do you really believe we could win, or even survive that? Against experienced combat troops? I said it was a stupid idea all along. You want to go try to get past that monster? No, we go back and live to fight another day."

"Yeah, you're right, Martin," said Officer Gomez. "I'm not going anywhere near that monster again. I'll quit first. Let's get the hell out of here." They set out but hadn't gone far when he spoke again. "Hey guys, listen."

A moment later Officer Kelly spoke. "I don't hear anything."

"That's right, Kelly," said Martin. "No gunfire, no screams, and no voices on the radio calling for the wagon or an ambulance. It's all over. Our guys are all dead. Keep moving."

While Martin led his fellow officers out of the sewers, Tasha sped towards the sound of gunfire. She heard a soft moan of pain as she passed the beast's lair. "More," it begged weakly.

"Later, I promise," she replied as she continued on her way.

Tasha soon came up behind the few remaining police. She grabbed one and threw him out into the line of fire. A second turned to shoot at her, but she was inside his reach instantly, her knife plunging deeply. She dropped his body and made a rolling dive away as the Lieutenant sprayed gunfire in her direction. She came up, her side arm at the ready, but there was no need.

Decoy kicked away the dead man's body and stepped to the next post of cover. He paused for a heartbeat then made a rolling dive across the open area, spraying lead as he went. There was a cry of pain then silence. Soon Intel called out. "Report!"

Shouts of "Clear," echoed through the tunnels. It was over.

"Lady Justice?"

"Here, Intel."

"All right, men. Injuries? Casualties?"

"We lost two men and have five wounded by my count, Sir," reported Finder.

"The wounds?"

"None serious."

"Very good. All right, men. Gather their weapons and anything else of value then dispose of the bodies."

"What about our guys?" asked a voice.

"There's a cemetery two blocks away," replied Intel. "We'll take them there. We'll see it done right. Wrap them up now, bring their gear. They'll take it with them to the next life. Decoy, check the tunnels, make sure we didn't miss any."

"Sir."

"Wait," said Tasha. "I'll do that. I pulled three out before the shit hit the fan. Maybe Decoy could make sure they don't get lost down here."

Intel grinned and nodded. Decoy trotted away, carefully avoiding the lair of the beast. "Finder."

"Yes Boss?"

"Is there any chance at all you could magically produce a tin whistle, flute, pan pipes, or such?"

"Got just the think back at headquarters, Lady J. What's up?"

"The beast got shot up pretty bad. I just thought I would give him a bit more music in case he doesn't make it."

"Boss?"

"He a child, Intel. No matter what he is, mentally he's just a child. I know he's dangerous, but he took out half that team before they got to you. Don't we owe him something, a little music at least?"

"The thing's an unknown entity, Lady J. It's savage, dangerous, and god knows what else. I don't like having it so close to us all the time." He sighed and let his shoulders slump. "But, as you say, he did half the job for us and probably saved a lot of our lives. Just promise to be careful and don't get too close."

"I won't."

"Don't get too attached either."

"What?"

"In combat situations attachments to the enemy, or civilians in the combat zone, can cost you your life and the lives of your fellow soldiers."

"You're right, Intel. I know it. I won't get attached, but I don't think he can survive. He sounded so terribly weak. I just wanted to..."

Finder reappeared and passed her a Native American flute. "Will this do, Boss?"

"Perfect, Finder. Thanks. I'll meet you guys back at headquarters."

She slipped swiftly along the now familiar pathway towards the beast's lair. She looked slightly puzzled as there seemed to be a dead body missing. When she reached the lair every body that had been lying about was gone. The beast had cleaned up his own house. Tasha shook her head.

"I see you." The voice was horribly weak, barely more than a whisper.

"I know. I see you too."

"More."

"Yes. More." She put her back against the wall and slowly slid down to a seated position. Raising the flute to her lips, she began to play a soft haunting melody.

"Yesssss," the voice breathed, then fell silent.

Tasha played and played. Time passed and she finally stopped. She waited, but there was no demand for more. With a strange sadness, she rose and returned to headquarters.

The Aftermath

Jessica Logan knew she had company the instant she entered the apartment. "Thank god she's alive," was her first thought. She kicked off her shoes and silently headed to the bedroom. There on her bed was a sleeping Lady Justice, a crude and bloodied bandage on her arm. Her gasp alerted Tasha who fought the sleep and spoke.

"Jess?"

"It's me, Tash. You're hurt."

"It's okay, probably healed already. I just hope it missed my tattoo. Sorry about making such a mess of the place, I..guess I fell asleep."

"When was the last time you slept?"

"When was I here last?"

"Dammit, girl, you have to start taking better care of yourself. Strip off now and get in that shower. You need a bath then ten hours sleep. We'll follow that with a meal and you'll be good as new." As she spoke, Jessica had removed Tasha's bandage to see a fresh scar where a bullet wound had been recently.

She helped Tasha to her feet then started stripping off her clothes. Tasha gave a small grin but put up no resistance. "What are you grinning at?"

"Like what you see, Jess?"

"What? Why you..."

"Come on, Jess. Get in the shower with me. You know you want to."

"Tasha..."

"Come on." Tasha smiled dreamily, taking Jessica by the hand and leading her toward the bathroom.

Jessica sighed then stripped off while Tasha started the shower. As soon as they stepped into the warm water Tasha melted into Jessica's arms. The kiss didn't happen. Jessica felt the trembling and weakness in the woman she held. "Aw, Tash," she sighed as she gently stood Tasha back up then proceeded to bathe her and wash her hair.

Once out of the shower Jessica dried Tasha off, wrapped her hair in a towel turban then led her back to the bed. She tucked her in then crawled in beside her. Tasha was asleep almost before Jessica cuddled her close. With a soft smile and a kiss for Tasha's forehead, Jessica closed her eyes and went to sleep.

Several hours later Jessica awakened with Tasha sleeping soundly in her arms. She lightly kissed the girl's hair then slipped out of the bed without waking the sleeping beauty. She relieved herself then headed for the kitchen. "I know what will bring you around, my warrior princess." She began to sing softly as she started cooking breakfast.

The food was nearly ready before she heard the soft harmony to her song. "I thought this would get your attention."

Tasha yawned as she snuggled deeper into Jessica's robe and approached the table. "Gods, Jess, you know I love your cooking."

"Yep, the way to a warrior's heart is through her stomach."

"You're not wrong. Jess, about last night..."

"Oh Tasha, that was so amazing. I've never been kissed like that and I think I broke something I orgasmed so hard."

"Shit, I fell asleep on you, didn't I?"

Jessica chuckled as she served breakfast. "You did, honey. Tash, you were so tired. I've never seen you like that. I'll admit I nearly freaked when I saw the bloody bandage."

"Not to worry, pretty lady, it completely missed my tattoo. See?"

"So I see. Well, thank god for that. Otherwise I'd have to find a new girlfriend."

"Jess, abut that."

"I'm being pushy?"

"You're being crazy. First, think of who I am and what would happen if anybody found out."

"Yeah, I guess that could get awkward."

"Second, I'm straight, at least I used to be."

"Used to be?"

"Yeah, but I have a hunch Moragah changed more about me than I have yet discovered."

"What do you mean?"

"I mean Intel is the kind of guy that would have floated my boat a while ago and now I can't see past the cook."

"Well, that sounds encouraging."

"Jess?"

"Mmm?"

"I came on to you last night, didn't I?"

"Yep, then promptly fell asleep in my arms."

"Big let down, huh."

"Yes and no. It was sweet and I enjoyed holding you. Tash, I think you need a bit more time to sort yourself out."

"Yeah, you're not wrong there. Jess, if you find..."

"Shut up, Tasha. Sort yourself out. I'll still be here when you're sure one way or another. We'll see what happens from there."

"Okay, if you're sure."

"I'm sure. Now, tell me what the hell Martin was babbling about when he got back to the station? Something about a monster?"

"There's something not quite human down in the sewers. It's big, strong, and lightning fast. I have no idea why Martin is going on about it, I pulled him out before he saw it. The other two saw it. It ripped into the police like a hurricane, but it took a number of wounds. I doubt it survived. It was pretty weak last time I spoke with it."

"You talked to it? What is it?"

"Alone? Are you crazy?"

"No, listen. I won't go
military escort. I'll go into
want. Maybe they'll help."

"Why would they do th

"Chief, they had the ch
we did that sweep search f
their leader seemed like a rea
soldier who will let me find
let him know I'm coming an
information."

"You know, Logan, tha
information from that area
man's name is Intel. Ask for
he said."

Jessica parked the polic
ragged fatigues watching h
walked right up to him.

"Hey there."

"Hey yourself."

"I'm looking for a man r
him?"

"Not sure, sometimes he

"All right. I'll go over to
cup and take my time with i
"Tell him all I want is inform
away. When she looked back

Jessica bought two co
window. Hers was only hali
moved with authority, and
coffee," she said, indicating h

He slid easily into a chai

"I don't know, it doesn't either. It's really child-like, Jess, but it's dangerous."

"What about the rest of the men?"

"All dead. They ran into the soldiers as they escaped the beast. Those men aren't coming back. Now, I need to know what happened topside while the war was on."

"Not much I can tell you. The commissioner demanded a full-scale attack on the military zone. The chief refused to lead it, so the Lieutenant jumped at it. The commissioner promised him the chief's job if he could bring back your head. There were reports of gunfire down in the zone, but Martin, Kelly and Gomez were the only ones who came back."

"They're all that ever will. Dammit, this whole thing is pissing me off. My dad risked his life to gather enough evidence to put the mayor and commissioner away for years. Why the hell is the mayor out on bail and why the hell was the commissioner not charged? If the District Attorney's Office had done their job those men would still be alive."

"It's a strange world we live in. Can I ask what sort of evidence your dad gathered?"

"Oh crap, Jess, I haven't kept you in the loop. So much has happened so fast. Okay, here's where things stand right now..."

Jessica sat quietly and listened while Tasha brought her up to speed. "Wow, so that's what's been going on. I always wondered why the commissioner's bully boys went after your folks. Now, this girl, this daughter, what's that all about?"

"Almost a side issue, but it made me start digging deeper. Once I met her and got her story I thought I had the reason Dad and Mom were killed, but something still didn't add up."

Jessica's phone suddenly began to buzz. She glanced at it then went pale. "Oh shit."

"What? What is it, Jess?"

"I've been called b…
now so shorthanded. Ta
missing men."

"The hell you are…"

"No choice, honey."

"I'll meet you down
bedroom in a heartb…
blood-stained fatigues, s
a quick kiss on the cheel

Jessica arrived at th
subdued. She swiftly ch
briefing room. Half th
there, as was the chief. It

"Pay attention peo…
officers was sent into the
Fifteen officers went in.
sat looking at their hand
monster, Lady Justice, a…
is, we have no real idea v

"Now, here's what's
man who brought the o…
down into the sewers to
o'clock this morning five
outside the city. They w…
rest of them."

Jessica stood up and
"Go ahead, Logan."

"Chief, I think our
in question lies with the
more people down into

"And you've got a be

"Sir, let me go in alo

"Yep. The chief said if we need information from this zone we should ask you."

"What's your name, Officer?"

"Jessica Logan."

He nodded. "I thought it might be you. Our mutual friend said you'd be coming. I was expecting you to take a different route."

"Yeah. I talked them out of that one. It can be dangerous."

"Oh yes, indeed it can. So, how can I help, Officer Logan?"

"Jess. My friends call me Jess, and since we're practically family…"

"Thanks, Jess. I'm just Intel. Freddy's dead, so the government says. So, again I ask, how can I help?"

"It seems a few officers got lost in the sewers near here last night, Intel. I was hoping you and your men might know what happened to them."

"Oh?"

"Look, I'm not here to investigate or gather evidence. I just want to know if anybody is coming home."

"Unless Lady J took them out last night, they're not coming back. The rules stand. You bring harm here; you don't go home."

"Understood. Is there anything left I could take back? ID, or anything else like that?"

He nodded then took out his phone. He tapped out a message then dropped the phone back into his pocket. "I'll give you what I've got," he said after a long sip of the coffee. "I'll keep the weapons and such, but you'll get the IDs and personal effects, at least most of them."

"Most of them?"

"Jess, there's something else in those sewers besides rats. We don't know what it is, but it is bloody dangerous. Last night it took out half your people. There will be gaps in what I give you. That's why."

"Understood."

"Oh, I'm supposed to tell you, our friend got delayed. She says she'll catch up with you later." His phone buzzed. He glanced at it then dropped it back in the pocket. "Come on, let's go for a walk."

"Where are we going?" she asked once they were outside.

"Someplace I want you to forget you ever saw, but Lady J wants you to know how to reach if you ever need to."

"Got it," replied Jessica as they turned into an alley then disappeared through a broken piece of wall.

Down and down they went until they arrived at headquarters. She looked around and saw a huge room filled with military equipment, soldiers, and weapons. "Wow, you guys are way more organized and equipped than we realized."

Intel just grinned. They approached the old subway car, and he stopped beside the altar. "For Moragah. For Justice." He then led her inside. There was a table set against the wall with helmets, badges, wallets etc. spread out on it. "This all of it, Decoy?"

"All I could find, Sarge. I've got about nine different units here."

"There were fifteen officers sent in last night," said Jessica. "Three returned. That leave twelve unaccounted for."

"Well, Ma'am, I've got nine here for sure, but there's something you should know."

"Oh?"

"There's something else down here that lives in the sewers. We don't know what it is, but it's deadly. It accounted for a number of your people, but I didn't try searching its lair."

"There's nothing there to find," said Tasha as she came in, tucking her flute into her belt.

"So, it's still alive," said Intel.

"Yeah, he's still alive. Look, Intel, I know you'd be happier if I just killed it, but where's the justice in that? He was content to live there in the water until we humans all started stomping around in his home. He defended himself against home invaders. I..."

"Easy, Boss, easy. I know you're right. Whatever he is, he's not the bad guy here. We are, from his point of view. It's just that he's a dangerous unknown entity and he makes me nervous."

"I know. Sorry to go off on you. Hi, Jess. I couldn't find anything in his lair. He cleaned up pretty good, considering he's all shot to pieces. I have to say, I didn't expect you to come in alone and by the topside route."

"Yeah, well, I thought I had better chances of not getting shot all to hell if I did it this way."

"That was good thinking," grinned Intel. "Come on, Officer Logan. I'll help you carry this back to your cruiser."

While Intel took Jessica back to her car, Tasha turned to the rest of the men. "Guys, everything okay here?"

"We're all good, Boss," replied Decoy. "You on the way out?"

"Yeah, I've got business topside."

"Watch your back, Boss."

Tasha smiled as she left. The next stop would be the police chief's house.

Marsha met her husband at the door when he arrived home from work. "Carl, welcome home. Dinner's on the table and we have a guest. You'd better hurry before she eats us out of house and home."

"I heard that," called Tasha. The chief found her seated at the table, waiting for her hosts. It was obvious she and his wife had gotten past their differences. Once the chief and his wife were seated, Tasha dove in again. "Mmm, Marsha, this is divine. You really have to give J...me this recipe."

"Huh," said the chief. "So it is Logan who's your contact in the department. Girlfriend too, I'll bet."

Tasha had gone deathly still, her eyes cold and dangerous. "Chief..."

"Relax, Lady Justice. We're both off the clock here."

"How'd you guess? What gave it away?"

"Logan volunteered to go down to the military zone alone. No one in their right mind would do that unless she had a contact there. So, she can cook too can she?"

Tasha eyed him carefully for a moment then slowly relaxed. "Yep. Marsha has competition in the kitchen all right, but this is to die for."

"Look, Kid, I've been doing a lot of soul searching since you came here the first time. I'll admit I turned a blind eye from time to time in the past to preserve the peace and to keep my job. Not proud of any of it. I know what you've done, and I know why. Your secret is safe with me. So is Logan. Don't tell her, but she's getting promoted to Lieutenant as soon as the commissioner is behind bars."

"So, you saw the evidence?"

"Yeah, Murdock brought that memory stick with him. Man, those vile money-grubbing bastards."

"So why the hell isn't the commissioner behind bars right now?"

"The D.A. Wouldn't prosecute. Don't know why."

"You won't mind if I ask him, will you?"

"Not at all, as long I don't know anything about it."

"Works for me. What about the mayor, is he going to get off?"

"Hard to say, but it'll drag out in the courts for years with appeal after appeal. It'll be a long time before he sees any jail time."

"You're spoiling my dinner, Chief."

"Sorry."

"At least his political career is ruined."

"Wouldn't count on it."

"Aw come on." Tasha sat bolt upright; her eyes ablaze.

The chief laid down his fork and sat back in his chair. "I won't lie to you, Kid. Not now, not ever. This is how it works for the rich guys. If you can prove they gave the kill order on your family, we might get lucky, otherwise..."

"This is wrong on so many levels."

"Yes it is and it makes me crazy too," said the chief. "Forgive me for saying it, and this goes no further than this room, but if there's going to be any justice in this, it'll be up to you to make it happen."

"I can live with that," said Tasha, poking at the food on her plate.

"Stop this, both of you," said Marsha. "You're ruining a perfectly good dinner with all this talk. I insist you discuss something more upbeat at the table."

Tasha gave her a sheepish look. "You're right, Marsha. My bad, I started it. So, Chief, you're going to promote Jessica?"

"Yes. I offered it to Murdock, but he said no. He's still planning to retire soon. He took the open sergeant's position. Said it was more his speed."

"That's so great. With Jess and Bill Murdock to back you it'll be easier to weed out the bully boys."

"That is my hope."

"They'll still keep hunting you, Tasha, you know that," said Marsha.

"I know, but that's okay. I've known that all along. I just want this city to be safe again. Marsha, thanks for the meal and the chat this afternoon. I enjoyed both more than you know. I have to go now."

"People to see, things to do?"

"Yes Ma'am, all that sort of stuff."

"Be careful, Tasha."

"Will do. Later, Chief." Marsha saw her to the door then sighed in wonder as Tasha seemed to just disappear into the night.

Trap

It took nearly an hour to reach the DA's house. As Tasha cautiously approached the gate her instincts began to scream of danger. Redoubling her efforts at stealth she leaped the gate and slunk along the hedge that lined the long driveway. Her instincts went off the scale and she stopped, trembling in fear.

She took a deep breath and released it slowly. Using all her visual powers she took in every square inch of the area. Something caught her attention and she focused on it. Invisible light beams. She was standing in a spiderweb of them. "Moragah?"

"*Run!*" She ran. Shifting onto combat mode, Tasha made a break for the gate and the streets beyond. Fast as she was, she couldn't outrun a bullet. She cried out at the shock of the bullets entering her back and leg. Tasha stumbled and fell but regained her feet just as a jeep blasted through the gates. She turned to run from that, but another bullet tore into her side and again she fell.

Tasha rolled away and saw a small missile shoot past her. Horrified she saw it turn and start back. Heat seeker. Before she could move a gout of flame leaped to life ten feet away from her and the missile exploded in it. The shouting men racing toward her were suddenly blocked by a wall of dancing flames.

"Can you walk?" A small figure dressed in black with blue spirals on her face tried to help her up. Tasha tried to respond, but melted back towards the ground. The small one scooped her up like a rag doll and ran with the wounded woman in her arms. She stuffed Tasha into the jeep then leaped behind the wheel.

They spun around and with a squeal of tortured rubber, sped away. "Where?" Weakly, Tasha tried to point the way. The jeep sped through the streets at desperate speed. They were near the military zone when the police car gave chase. The driver ignored it, continuing her race to safety.

The jeep screeched to a halt and was instantly surrounded by armed soldiers. The driver ignored them, slapping aside one man's rifle as she raced around the jeep and gently lifted Tasha out. "Stop the cops." With that she started unerringly towards the path down to headquarters.

"I've got her," said a big man as he stepped into her path and gently took her burden. "This way. You men, send those cops home one way or another." A few short moments later they were in the old subway car. He laid Tasha gently on a bed of cardboard and the small woman sat beside her, gathering Tasha into her arms. "What do you need, ma'am?"

"Bandages and privacy." The bandages instantly appeared and another man began issuing orders.

The car was immediately abandoned to the tiny healer in blue war paint. "Lady Moragah."

"I am here, Kara. Hold Tasha gently now and I will heal her wounds." Every man in the immediate area felt the flow of healing energy as Moragah restored her priestess. It took time, for Tasha hovered on the edge of the abyss. She had lost considerable blood. Finally her wounds squeezed out the offending bullets then sealed over. Her labored breathing grew steadily deeper until she was sleeping peacefully.

Kara grabbed a nearby blanket to cover her then went outside where the men were gathered. "She's sleeping now," she said as she sat on the steps and drew a deep relaxing breath. "She'll be fine in a few days."

"What happened?" The man before her was the one who had been barking orders. Obviously the commander.

"What happened? You guys fucked up, that's what happened. You're supposed to be her protectors, but you're hiding down here like scared rats..." She stopped and tilted her head, as though listening. "You're right, Lady Moragah, not these guys' fault. Sorry guys, I'm just really bummed that I was almost too late."

"You're Lady Blue, aren't you? The one called Kara. Lady J told us about you. I'm Intel. All I can say is thank Moragah you arrived in time."

"That was too close for comfort," replied Kara. "Okay, Moragah says to bring you up to speed. I was on my way west when Moragah called me to turn around. I broke every speed record getting here. Moragah directed me to a house, gated. There was gunfire inside and I saw Tasha fall. I busted in, lit the place up and brought her out."

"Why didn't you take her to a hospital?" asked one of the men.

"She'd have died. I knew Moragah could heal her if I could just get to a place of safety where she could work. Tasha pointed the way here and Moragah told me about you guys while I drove." She turned her head and listened again, nodded then went on.

"Apparently something has gone sideways, and the DA has the answers. Tasha was on her way to ask him a few pointed questions when she blundered into a nest of paramilitary guards. This guy is seriously paranoid. She must have tripped a silent alarm. By the time she realized it she was in a war zone. She took five bullets. One in the back, side, one in the leg, a graze on her noggin, and this one will really piss her off. One through the tattoo on her shoulder." A relieved group of soldiers grinned at that.

Suddenly there was a fuss as Alicia Murdock came pushing her way through the press of men. "Someone said Tasha's been hurt. What happened? Is she all right? Can I talk to her? What...?

Kara just grinned and shook her head. "Come here, gorgeous, sit beside me and I'll tell you what I can." With a blush on her cheeks Alicia sate beside Lady Blue. "Okay, Tasha got shot, but Moragah healed her. She's going to be fine in a couple of days. So, no need to panic."

"Oh thank god."

"So who are you, pretty lady? You Tasha's girlfriend?"

Alicia smiled and blushed again. "I thought about it once or twice, but it wasn't happening. No, I'm just a friend and a reporter who owes her everything."

"Girl, there's no such thing as just a friend in our world. The servants of Moragah don't make a lot of friends and we cherish the ones we do. You'd be the one who did the interview that started her wearing that Halloween costume."

"Hey..."

"Relax, I know the plan behind it, and it's a good one, but I've got a way better idea. It starts with a kevlar vest and a camo uniform with the scales of Justice on the chest. Add a few blue spirals and you're ready to go."

"I've been trying to get her to wear armor," said Intel. He was interrupted by a weak voice from inside the car.

"Guys, I need my phone..."

Kara's head snapped around. "Your phone? You don't need a damn phone, you need rest. Go back to sleep."

"I gotta call Jess..."

"You've got to sleep. Tasha don't make me come back in there, cause if I do you'll sleep and then some."

"Oh sure, go all tough butch on me when I'm all shot up. You just wait until I'm on my feet again, then we'll see what happens."

"I'll set your britches on fire; that's what'll happen. Now go back to sleep." Kara winked at Intel as she rose and went back inside. She took the remains of the phone and brought it to Tasha. "Sorry, it got shot."

"Dammit, that's the second phone I've lost like that this year."

"Need to call a girlfriend?"

"She's not...we haven't quite got there yet, and I don't think we should."

"Honey, save some of that for later, and take my advice, let the girl make up her own mind. Right now, you need another ten hours sleep then a rare steak or two to get your blood back up." She smiled warmly as she patted Tasha's shoulder. "Do this for me. I didn't risk my life to save your sorry butt just to have you cash in by chasing the girls."

"All right, Mamma Kara, but I heard Alicia out there. Will you ask her to go to Jess and tell her I'm all right?"

"Will you promise to rest."

"Word of honor."

"Deal." Kara tucked the blanket around Tasha again then stepped back outside.

"Alicia, do you know this Jess she's hung up on?"

"Yes, I do. Want me to go set her mind to rest?"

"Yeah, that would be good. Me and the boys here have another errand."

Intel's ears perked up at that. "We going someplace, Lady Blue?"

"We are. Leave a few trusted folk here to care for her then pick a few men who aren't afraid of.."

"No one here's afraid, Blue. Combat vets, every last one of us."

"Sorry. Bring as many as you can fit into my jeep and let's go."

JESSICA LOGAN WAS PACING. Something was wrong. Tasha should have arrived hours ago, and she wasn't answering her phone. The sound of the buzzer made her jump. "Dammit, someone's at the door." She stepped to the intercom. "What?"

"Are you Jessica Logan?"

"What of it?"

"I'm Alicia Murdock. I have news of a mutual friend. May I come in?" The buzzer sounded and Alicia stepped through. Jessica was waiting for her at the top of the stairs.

"Come in, quickly." She hustled Alicia inside then shut the door tightly. "What happened? Is she all right?"

"She was shot, Jessica..."

"Oh god..."

"Hey, she's okay, she's okay." Alicia gathered the distraught woman into her arms to comfort her. "She's okay. It was bad, really bad, but Lady Blue was there and brought her out. She took her to headquarters and healed her. Tasha will be fine, but she needs a few days rest. That's all, just a few days rest."

Jessica was sobbing. "I knew when she didn't answer her phone..."

"That got shot too. She's pissed about that cause she wanted to call you."

Jessica stepped back and dried her eyes. "I have to go to her. I..."

"You can't Jessica, you can't. If you do your career is over. They'll know and they'll know you're the contact on the police force. You'll be thrown in jail for abetting a murderer. Think, girl, think. You'll be no good to her behind bars. I'll get her a new phone so you guys can talk, but right now she needs rest, and you need a drink."

Jessica nodded her head slowly. "Have a drink with me? After all, we've been co-conspirators for a while now. It's time we got to know each other."

Alicia smiled and nodded. "I don't usually drink, but, sure, why not. Dang fine idea."

"You sit," said Jessica, waving at the sofa. She went to the cupboard looked inside for a moment, then shook her head. "I'm afraid we're on the hard stuff tonight."

"Oh?"

"Yep. Nothing in the house but ginger ale."

Alicia laughed. "Works for me. So tell me, how did you and Tasha meet?"

"Me and Tash, I want to hear how you met her."

"Me? That's an easy one. She came to the house to kill my dad. He talked her out of it."

"Wait, wait. I want to hear all of this one. Old grouchy Bill actually talked her out of it? Oh this is going to be good." She passed Alicia a glass then sat near her on the couch. "Go on." Over the next few hours life stories were exchanged, a friendship was forged, and Jessica's mind was put at ease.

While Jessica was getting a drink for Alicia, the DA was getting more visitors. His alarms sounded again, but this time it was different. A jeep blasted past the broken gate and charged at the house. By the time the guards got to the door a band of heavily armed soldiers were pouring out of the jeep. Several shots were fired then the soldiers were in the house and the guards were down.

A small woman with blue spirals on her face was shouting orders. "Find him. Find him but keep him alive for me."

The soldiers spread out through the house. Soon calls of "Clear!" began to ring out. The house was searched, but no one was found. "There's got to be a panic room somewhere," said Lady Blue. "I was in enough of those before Penny found me. Be quiet now and let me listen."

Not a breath was heard as she listened, turning her head this way and that, slowly moving from room to room. She made her way to the basement, to a bookcase then smiled. "Bingo." She grabbed the case and ripped it away from the wall, exposing a door hidden behind it. "Ready? On three. One, two, three." On three she kicked the heavy door from the hinges and the troops stormed inside.

There were screams of terror and shouts as the men captured the DA and his family. He was cowering on the floor beside his wife and children. Kara marched up to him, grabbed him by the shirt front and hauled him up to go nose to nose with him. "I want answers and you'd better be in the mood to sing."

"I won't tell you anything. I..."

She slapped him, knocking him back onto the floor. "Take the woman and children outside. If I yell fire, kill one. I don't care which one. We'll keep going until this idiot talks."

"Noooo," screamed the DA, but a big boot jammed him face first on the floor and a gun barrel was put to his head. "Shut the fuck up," growled a deep voice. Kara winked at Intel and he roughly hauled the woman to her feet then herded her and the two children up the stairs and outside.

"Please," she begged as they passed the dead guards.

"Please what?"

"Please don't kill us."

"Okay. I won't."

"What?" Just then the call came from the basement. "Fire!"

He fired a shot into a tree and grinned. "Sorry ma'am. The idea here is to loosen your husband's tongue, that's all."

"But the guards..."

"A friend of mine came here tonight to ask a few questions. She was shot, nearly died. Your man has gone to great expense to hide and protect something. We want to know what that is. Now, the next time I fire a shot, I want you to scream."

"What? Why?"

"It'll make it sound more authentic. Ma'am, I don't want to hurt you or the kids. All we ever wanted was information, but we were greeted with bullets. This time we came prepared. We won't leave without the information."

"Fire!" Intel shot the tree again. The woman screamed.

"Nice one. That should do the trick."

"If he doesn't talk are you going to kill him?"

"Nope. If Lady Blue can't get the information out of him we'll take him to Lady Justice."

She turned and screamed into the house. "Arnold, please..." It was heart wrenching and Intel raised an eyebrow. A few moments later the DA came through the door, his head hanging low. He was startled to see both his children alive.

He turned to his wife, but Intel stepped between them. "In fairness to your wife, Sir. I did threaten to rape her and kill the children while she watched. She did what she had to do to protect them and herself. She's a strong and resourceful woman. You're a lucky man."

"Yeah, lucky man. So now you're going to kill me?"

"Nope," replied Kara. "We've got what we came for. We'll deliver the information to Lady Justice. What she does from there is up to her. If I were you, Arnold, I'd head for Mexico and never look back. Have a good night folks." She and her troops piled into the jeep, and it raced away from his house for the second time that night.

ALICIA ARRIVED BACK headquarters. It was nearly dawn. Tasha was sleeping peacefully, and Kara was just returning, she looked tired. She pulled a recorder from her pocket and tossed it to Alicia. "It's all there, girl. Thanks for the loan of the recorder."

"My pleasure."

"I'll let you make sense of all that. Tasha will want a sensible version when she wakes up. Intel, you promised me a bed."

"Yes Ma'am. Can you sleep on cardboard?"

"Just watch me," sighed Kara as she sank onto the makeshift bed he pointed to. A moment later he gently laid a blanket over her sleeping form.

Piecing it Together

Kara awakened to hustle, bustle, and hushed voices all around. "Hey, what's all the racket?"

"Bout time you woke up," said Tasha. A big smile was on her face. "It's been over ten hours."

"Yeah, I was beat all right. You sleep any?"

"I did, Little Mamma. I did."

"So, where the latrines boys?"

"I'll show you," smiled a girl as she stepped forward.

"This is Amy," said Intel. "She's our girl Friday around here. We'd be lost without her." He saw the grin on Kara's face and shook his finger. "I don't want to hear it. Especially not in front of the troops."

Kara laughed as she followed Amy out the secret door and down to the washrooms by the subway platform. There were people there, but they paid the two women no attention at all. "Folks know there's stuff going on in the tunnels," said Amy as she noticed Kara's raised eyebrow. "They pretend to see nothing because their streets and homes are safe."

"You know, I like what I see going on here. I might just find a city of my own and settle down once this is over."

"Once this is over? Are you staying around for a while?"

"Yep, I am."

"Awesome."

"So, I got the impression you think Intel is pretty cute."

The girl blushed. "Does it show?"

"Oh yeah, it does."

They continued to chat as they returned to the hideout to find Tasha, Alicia, and Intel deep in conversation. "Hey, Kara," said Tasha, "How much do you know about what's going on?"

"Quite a bit after last night. Listen you, you're not going anywhere or doing anything until you've had a few days more rest. I'm staying right here to make sure you do as you're told."

"Kara?"

"Look, you got a bum deal here, and I'm sorry about that. You were left on your own and that shouldn't have happened. Sometimes life explodes all over the best of plans, even Moragah's.

"I was supposed to talk to you, wait until you made your choice, then guide you for a few months until you came into your own. That didn't happen. One day I'll tell you why, but for now, I'm here to help."

"You were sent to guide me?"

"Yep. Penny was the first Lady Blue. She had to learn on her own. It was tough and she came too close too many times. When I was made priestess I had Penny to guide me, so did Mai. It was my job to guide you, but I got called away."

"So there's four like you?" asked Intel.

"Three. Penny, me, and Tasha. That call away was for Mai, but she was dead before I got there. I turned back as soon as I knew. I got here just in time to prevent another disaster."

"Aw, Kara, I'm so sorry."

"Thanks, Tash. Look it is what it is and the way we live, that can happen to any of us at any time. I was too late in Vancouver, but not here. So, I'm here to help and guide you."

"Thanks, Kara. I can use all the help I can get."

"Then stop being so damn proud and independent. These men are awesome. Let them help you. Learn what they have to teach."

"Sure, go ahead and gang up on me when I'm all shot up. Intel's been preaching that at me for weeks."

"Listen to the man, Tasha. He's good at what he does."

Tasha nodded her agreement. "I know, and you're right, but what I do is so damn risky."

"You protect your people, I like that. So, enough chatter. What are we doing and who do I have to beat up?"

"Beat up?" asked Intel.

"People, listen carefully. My mandate is different from Tasha's. I can't take anyone out unless he comes at me or an innocent. She can, I can't. That's just how it works. Now, here's the bitter part. If we go after somebody and one of you gets too aggressive I have to stop you, maybe the hard way. Let that sink in a bit." The room was silent.

"So that's why you lead the charge last night," said Intel. "That's why you made us wait until one of them fired a shot. Sweet Jesus, Kid, you played that one tight."

"Yeah, well, it's kinda like that for me. We didn't have a lot of time to go into detail last night. Okay, enough of this. We're after the guys who ordered the hit on Tasha's parents, right? We know who it is, but we need more evidence, is that it?"

"No, I don't think I do," said Tasha, a cold deadly note in her voice. "I wanted to know why the DA wouldn't prosecute the commissioner. What else was going on that needed to be brought to light? Where the hell did he get that kind of security anyway? Hired guns don't come cheap."

"They were a gift from the commissioner," said Alicia as she entered to join them. "Hi Kara. Look, I've made a sensible copy of that interrogation, but there's not a damn bit of it that's admissible as evidence."

"I really don't care, Allie," said Tasha. "I just need to know."

"Okay, here goes. You already know what the mayor and the commissioner are up to. Here's where the DA fits in. He caught wind of their little rape gang tricks in college, gathered enough evidence to bring them to heel. He underestimated the commissioner who spent years watching until he finally got the goods on Mr. DA. It seems our upstanding prosecutor is an habitue of a certain gay BDSM club.

"The commissioner set him up, got film, and the rest is history."

"There's no honor at all among thieves," said Tasha. "Is the DA still alive?"

"Last I saw he was," replied Kara. "I told him to blow town and keep going; that you'd be coming for him soon."

"You weren't wrong on that count. Let's go..."

"Find someplace to relax," said Kara. "You're in no shape to go anywhere except to bed."

Tasha just shook her head. "All right, you bully. We'll go relax. You play a musical instrument?"

"Nope."

"Like music?"

"Sure."

"Okay, come on, we'll go entertain a friend."

"Aw Boss, not in the shape you're in."

"Relax, Intel. Lady Blue will be with me. Besides, he's all shot to hell just like me. It'll be fine."

"You're gonna be the death of me, woman. Blue, stay sharp, that thing is bloody dangerous."

"What thing?" asked Kara.

Tasha sighed as she pulled out her flute. "There's something down in the sewers. We don't know what it is. It doesn't know what it is. Intel's right, it's strong, fast, and its touch burns like hellfire. However, it's child-like and just wants to be left alone. It loves the flute, so I go play for it.

"A few nights ago the police stormed the sewers looking for us. The beast cleaned out half of them but got shot up in the process. Somehow it's still alive, but in a lot of pain.

"I doubt I could heal it, don't think I want to, but the music brings it some peace. I owe it that much. I don't dare go down there in the shape I'm in right now, but if you came with me..."

"Okay, so I'm the bodyguard. Cool, let's go." As they left the subway car a big soldier passed Kara an automatic rifle. She nodded her thanks and slung it over her shoulder. Tasha saw but said nothing. She led the way along the sewer tunnels.

"Almost there," said Tasha as she stopped and reached out with her hearing. It was still there, she could hear it moving in the water, its raspy breathing. She listened for a moment then looked perplexed. "His breathing sounds a bit better. The big guy might just survive." she moved on slowly, carefully.

"I see you."

"I know. I brought a friend."

"Friend?"

"Friend. No harm."

"Friend. I see you."

"I see you too, big guy," replied Kara.

"Why carry pain stick?"

Kara pondered for a moment then removed the rifle and slid it away towards the entrance to the lair. She spread her arms wide then sat carefully beside Tasha.

The beast sighed then drew a long ragged breath. "More."

"Yes. More." Tasha began to play. The music was soothing, but Kara never once relaxed. After a long while Tasha stopped playing.

"More."

"I have to go now. More later." She started away and Kara scooped up the rifle as she followed.

"Lady Justice." Tasha froze in place, her heart racing, and every nerve on full alert. Slowly, carefully she turned to where a huge form moved in the water. "My name is Dan."

Tasha swallowed hard then replied. "Good to know you, Dan. I'll come back later and play more."

"Thank you," sighed the voice then it was silent.

Tasha wasted no time in getting back to the headquarters. She and Kara stopped at the altar. "For Moragah, for Justice." Kara smiled with delight as she repeated the prayer then followed Tasha inside.

Intel took one look at Tasha's face and went serious. "What?"

"His name is Dan," she replied.

"Who's name is Dan?"

"The beast."

"Talk to me, Boss."

"Up until now he has been completely child-like, barely able to get out a word or two."

"And?"

"Today he seemed like he's recovering. As we were leaving he called me by name then told me his name is Dan. We know he absorbs life force and information from whatever he eats. The other night he killed five policemen then the bodies disappeared."

"Oh fuck. Decoy!"

A head appeared in the doorway. "Sarge?"

"Double the guards on every possible route from the beast's lair to here. Make sure those men stay alert."

"Sir!" The man's head disappeared then returned a moment later, followed by the body as Decoy returned. "What's up?"

Tasha spoke up. "The beast is recovering and he's getting smarter, a lot smarter. He must have eaten some of those he killed the other night."

"And?"

"He absorbs knowledge and strength from whatever he eats."

"So, if he ate a dead cop he would learn language?"

"Yes, and?"

"Full understanding of what a weapon is and how to use it. Fuck." Decoy disappeared again.

"I'm not happy about this, Boss," said Intel. "Not one little bit."

"Me either, Intel," said Tasha. "However, we've never harmed him, and he likes my music. Maybe he can become an ally."

"You'll forgive me if I don't count on that."

"Me either, good buddy, me either."

"Okay, so what happens now?" asked Kara.

"I catch a nap while you get interviewed by Alicia," replied Tasha.

"Hey, Lady Blue doesn't give interviews," replied Kara.

"Aw, why not?" asked Alicia.

"Well, to start with it will tell them what city I'm in. Jesus, what's wrong with you people? Why don't you just take out an advertisement. Hey, it's me, the killer, I'm down here."

"Woman's not entirely wrong, Boss," said Intel. "We could do with tightening things up a little."

"We'll work on it," replied Tasha. She sighed as she noticed Kara talking to Finder. "Now what's she up to?"

"I have no idea at all."

"The hell you don't, Intel," replied Tasha. "Fine, if you're all going to plot against me, I'm going for a nap." He nodded, noticing how tired she was. He signaled for everyone to quiet down and they all filed out of the old car.

"So, you're the guy they call Finder," said Kara.

"Yes ma'am. If it exists I can probably find it, given time. Is there something you need?"

"Yeah. I need fatigues and body armor to fit Tasha. You know what I mean."

"Yes Ma'am, I do. Might I suggest some for you too?"

"They make this shit in kid's sizes?"

He laughed softly. "You're not that small. Let me see what I can find."

Kara smiled in return. "Don't take too long, my friend. I don't know how long I can hold her down. The people she's after play for keeps and they're waiting for her."

"Yes ma'am, I heard that." He gave her a quick salute then trotted off towards the subway entrance.

"He going shopping for armor?" asked Intel as he approached Kara. She just nodded. "Good."

WHILE TASHA NAPPED and Kara fended off Alicia's less than subtle attempts to wheedle an interview, Jessica Logan was getting another surprise. "Officer Logan, my office, now," called the chief as he stuck his head out the door then disappeared back inside again. Surprised and confused, she approached his office door and knocked lightly. "Come in and shut the door." She complied.

"Have a seat," said the chief as he settled himself in his chair. She sat then waited. He paused for a moment then went on. "Logan, we need to speak plainly here, no holding back and nothing hidden. Can you do that?"

"Chief?"

"Can you do that?"

"Yes, of course."

"All right then, here's the deal. The Lieutenant's job is open. I want to put you in that on a temporary basis."

"Sir?"

"You heard me, Jessica. I'd make it permanent, but the commissioner will raise hell. We have evidence that should convict him of several crimes. As soon as we get all that straightened out, I'll make it permanent."

"Ah, don't get me wrong, Chief, but shouldn't that job go to a more senior man?"

"There's only one I would trust with it, and he refused. He took the vacant sergeant's position. He said you're the woman for the job."

"Murdock. Wow. Chief, won't they try to bring in someone else from another precinct?"

"They can try, but it won't happen. Look, I know you're young, and need more experience, but I'm willing to mentor you on this job. Will you take it?"

"Wow, I ah, well I, ah, can I sleep on it?"

"Logan, there's another reason I want you on this job."

"Sir?"

"You're the direct link to Lady Justice. In this job you'll be able to keep her on top of things."

"Sir, I..."

She'd started to rise, but he waved her back into the chair. "Oh sit down, woman. She told me herself over dinner. Huh. Kid thinks you're a better cook than Marsha. Ha."

"Chief? What's going on here?"

"What's going on here, Officer Logan? We're both in a position of aiding and abetting a known felon, a cop killer. So, let's drop the pretense and get on with it. We both want to clean up this force, make it what it once was. Tasha wants to clean up the city, make it safe for everybody again. We all want that. I'm tired of fighting a corrupt system. I want this done and I'm willing to accept her help to get it done."

"Holy shit. Chief, if this is a setup, you've just admitted she knows where you live."

"Knows where I live? Hell, she and my wife are buddies. It's not a setup, Jessica. I'm on the level here, I need your help, and we never had this conversation."

"What conversation, chief? Oh, about the new job, when do I start?"

He sighed with relief and relaxed back in his chair. "Your office is right next door. Go move yourself in then call the sergeant in and bring him up to speed. Don't worry, he's on side."

"I know. Okay, so it's off to suit up for the crusade. What are you going to tell the commissioner?"

"Not a damn thing until he asks then I'll tell him it's a done deed. He can holler and bluster all he wants, but there's nothing he can do until I make it permanent. That will happen the instant he's gone from office.

"You know, you're good Logan. I just spilled my guts, gave you enough to have me put away for life, and you never admitted to a damn thing. Murdock was right, you're perfect for the job." She just grinned and slipped out the door, her phone in her hand. She was hoping Intel could pass on a message.

Hard Truth

J essica Logan was pacing around the apartment again. It had been
three days since her promotion and she still hadn't seen Tasha.
Worse yet, she'd been thinking hard and had come to a difficult
decision. She stopped and listened, her ear turned toward the
bedroom, but there was no sound. Nothing. She went back to her
pacing and fretting.

The sound of the buzzer nearly stopped her heart. With a gasp she
turned and, swearing like a sailor, reached for the intercom. "State your
business."

"Hey, Jess, it's Alli."

"Come on up."

She was waiting to usher Alicia in. "Sit, girl. Want something to
drink with alcohol in it?"

"I'd rather coffee, if I may."

"I'll make a new pot. So, what brings you here this time?"

"A pretty woman who serves awesome drinks."

Jessica laughed in spite of her mood. "You're a nut, Alli, you know
that. Come on now, what's up?"

"I brought you something. It's a recording of an interview with the
DA. The interview was conducted by Lady Blue. You wouldn't be able
to use it for evidence, but it will give you some insights."

"Lady Blue, the woman who saved Tasha? Shit. Is he still alive?"

"Far as I know. Blue tends to be less deadly than Justice, but not by
much. So, what's eating my favorite bartender?"

"Huh?"

"You're wound up tight as a drum. What's going on?"

"None of your damn business."

"Sure it is, I'm a reporter. Everything is my business."

Jessica sighed and shook her head. "It's personal."

"Trying to figure a way to break up with Tasha?"

"How the hell did you come to that conclusion?"

"You guys are too much alike and I'm good at reading people. You both will go to the wall to protect someone you love. You both know it's doomed if you get together. If anyone ever found out they could get to her through you. You could go to jail for a hundred years. She could be killed trying to rescue you. I could go on."

"Please don't."

"Sorry."

"No, you're right. You've only said what keeps running through my mind. Go ahead, she's officially single now. Good luck."

"Me? Oh hell no. We've almost gone there and stopped for all the above reasons. No girl, not me. Whatever Tasha is or has become, I will always be her friend and supporter, but that's all, because anything else would be too dangerous for both of us.

"Sadly, Jess, you're in the same boat."

"Yep, I guess I am. So here we are, the ex-girlfriends of Lady Justice. Hell, I didn't even get a kiss."

"Me neither. Now that really bites, doesn't it? Got any ice cream?"

Jessica laughed and gently punched Alicia on the arm. "You're a complete nut. Yes, I have a fresh tub. I'll bring it and two spoons." She brought them and they dug in. "She sent you here to soften me up, didn't she? She's going to break up with me, right?"

"Yeah, she cares for you, Jess. She wants to protect you."

"I know. You tell her I expect her to drop by for dinner once in a while."

"I will."

"And tell her to get a new phone. Oh hell, she already has one, doesn't she? Give me the number." Alicia took Jessica's phone and entered the number as Alicia two. Jessica tapped in a message. "Chicken. Sending Alli to do the dirty work."

A moment later she got a reply. "Busted. Sorry. Jess, you know we can't."

"I know. I was thinking the same thing."

"We okay?"

"We're cool. Dinner Thursday?"

"Awesome." Jessica gazed at the phone for a moment then dropped it on the couch.

"All good?" asked Alicia.

"Yeah, it's all good. It's a bit of a relief actually, getting it stopped before we got in too deep."

"Yeah, I get that."

"Alli, you sneaky beast, you're keeping me distracted. Where is she?"

"I'm not telling you that, you're a cop, for crying out loud."

"She's gone after them hasn't she?"

"I honestly don't know, Jess. Blue has been keeping her close to home while she heals, but tonight they went out together. Didn't say where, but we could both make an educated guess if we wanted to."

"I don't really want to, and I don't need to know. Hey, quit hogging the tub."

"THIS THE PLACE, TASH?"

"According to the address in the phone book, this is the place."

"I've got a bad feeling about this."

"Me too, trap?"

"Yep, trap," said Kara.

"Yeah, well, I've been there recently and didn't like it. I'd like to turn the tables on these guys for a change. Feeling up to a bit of excitement?"

"What's the plan?"

"I imagine they'll have a similar setup to the other guys. I'll go on stealth mode. You run through the electronic gadgets then lead a few of them away. That will give me a chance to slip in behind them."

"What abilities will you use?"

"What???"

"You heard me, what abilities will you use to get inside?"

"Okay, coach. I can hide in plain sight. I'll use that. I can open a lock by just thinking about it. I can use that. I can use super hearing to make sure a place is clear before I go in. I'm wearing armor as well. Will that do it?"

Kara nodded then turned and studied the layout before her. The house was well back from the street and gated. She noted every bush and tree. She noted the cameras mounted on the eaves as well as the ones hidden in the bushes. "Hide."

Tasha seemed to vanish and Kara scaled the fence to land in a crouch on the other side. She crept along the fence until she reached the gate house. There was a man inside, but he was unconscious before he was aware of her. She unlocked the gate and let it swing open. With the gate open Kara's escape route was assured. She came down off combat mode and made her run.

Darting swiftly up the driveway, Kara kept her eyes on the door. As soon as her enhanced vision saw the knob begin to turn she spun around and fled. The door jerked open and a hail of gunfire followed the fleeing figure. Five men burst from the house, guns drawn and gave chase. They nearly had her cornered when she shifted onto combat mode and disappeared from their view.

Back at the big house, Tasha was inside. As she slipped through the door she became aware of more guards inside. They seemed to be defending a room at the top of the stairs. She came into view, shot one then ran into the living room. Both guards abandoned their post and ran after her. "Which way?" asked one as they reached the empty room.

"Beats me," replied the other. "You go back and watch the door. I'll look for this one." His companion nodded then turned away. He left the room while the other, gun at the ready, began to carefully search the room. He leaped to point his gun behind the couch, but saw nothing. Tasha stepped away from the wall, her powerful arms encircled his neck, twisted savagely, then she lowered the body to the floor.

Slipping the man's gun into her belt, she vanished again. Tasha could hear the last man breathing. He was nervous, frightened, his hand shaking on the weapon. She suddenly appeared beside him and shot him with his partner's gun. Kicking aside the body, she tried the door. It was locked.

"Halverson, that you?" asked a voice from behind the door. A grunt was his answer. "What's the password?" Several shots penetrated the door and he sank lifeless to the floor.

The door was kicked in and a nightmare was inside. Moving at lightning speed she finished off the two remaining guards. Only the commissioner was left. "Please don't, Kid, please..."

"For the rape of Monisha Kells mother, for the attempt on the life of your daughter, Monisha Kells, and for the murder of my parents, Kelly and Jonah Stewart, you will now face Justice." He tried to beg, but she shot him and his body collapsed on the floor. "Justice is served."

Tasha turned to leave and saw Kara standing in the doorway. "Christ, Tasha, that was a little cold."

"Yeah, I'm like that sometimes."

"Hey, I'm not the enemy here. Tell me."

"It's what I do, Kara. The way Moragah wants it done, not in a hot passion of vengeance, but cold unfeeling justice. She did something to me so I don't come unglued until it's over. I'll be a bit freaked out by it when we get home and I relax."

"Remind me not to piss you off. Come on, let's blow this popsicle stand."

"All the guards dead?"

"Nope. Tash..."

"No, Kara, I'm not going to kill them. I just wondered."

"Three dead and two more unconscious. I can see your count. Are we done here?"

"Yes. Next for the Mayor, he was a part of it all." Kara nodded then shifted onto combat mode. Tasha followed. In moments they were outside the wall and aboard Kara's jeep. She drove swiftly away.

A few blocks further and they found the mayor's house empty. "They've probably got him at a safe house somewhere," said Tasha. "We've done all we can for tonight. Let's go home."

They didn't make it all the way. They were still a few blocks from the military zone when Tasha shouted. "Stop the car!" Even as she spoke Kara had seen what caught her eye. Two police cars were at the curb. Several officers were holding a man in the air, he wasn't struggling. He was crying. His pants had been pulled down, and he was being beaten. One cop held his head up by the hair and sprayed pepper spray into his face.

That's when Tasha and Kara hit them. Suddenly uniformed bodies were being tossed in all directions. Several went for their guns and died instantly, two lay on the ground, unconscious, and the man who had used the pepper spray was on his knees, begging for mercy. Tasha came down off combat mode, holding him by the hair.

Kara was comforting the victim. He was obviously a man with Down syndrome. She saw Tasha and the cold deadly look in her eye. "Lady Justice, don't."

"Why not, Blue? You saw what they did, what this one did. I won't allow that kind of brutality in my city." The crowd that had gathered round was hushed.

"Because he's asking you not to," replied Kara as she helped the victim to stand.

"Please don't hurt him," said the victim. "He didn't mean to hurt me. I did something bad."

"How about it, Lady Justice," asked Kara. "What good is justice without compassion?"

Tasha drew a deep breath then looked the victim in the eye. Slowly she softened and released her hold on the policeman. "Do you need a ride home?" she asked the victim. He nodded. Tasha hauled the policeman to his feet.

"All right, you. First you put this gentleman in your car, thank him for your life, then make sure he is safe at home. After that go directly to the police station and report what happened here. Mess with me and I'll hunt you down. Got it?"

"Yes ma'am."

"Then get busy. You people, stop gawking and taking pictures. Call the police station and get some help down here for the rest of these men. Some of them might still be alive." She turned back towards the jeep. "Come on, Blue. Let's go."

Kara helped the policeman get the victim into the cruiser then joined Tasha in the jeep. "You okay?" asked Tasha as Kara started the car.

"Yeah, I'm good. I'm beginning to see why you do things for keeps. I know what bullies are like; they'll never stop until you make them stop."

"Then why did you make me leave that one alive?"

"The victim was already traumatized enough. He honestly believes the police are good, that he must have done something bad, and seeing you kill that jerk would only have messed him up more. Sorry, didn't mean to embarrass you in public."

"No? But you think it would be okay to embarrass me in private?"

"Oh hell, yes."

Tasha chuckled softly. "Kara, I'm sorry if I freaked you out tonight."

"We're good, Tash. I have no problems with what we did tonight. I'm just used to making them come at me first."

"Yeah, well, I got my ass shot off when I tried that. By the way, I wasn't going to kill that asshat. He deserved a swift kick for what he did, but he didn't go for a gun. I had no real reason to kill him."

"But that guy at the house..."

"Was guilty of a dozen or more crimes including rape and murder. He and the mayor are behind a lot of the problems in this city, including the police brutality thing."

"I guess I owe you an apology. I need to trust you more."

"Thanks, Kara. Look, I know I'm different from you Ladies Blue, my purpose is different. My job is to hold back the darkness if I can, not add to it."

"Sounds like a fine line to walk."

"Yeah, it is, and it scares the bejebbers out of me sometimes."

"That why you don't like carrying a gun?"

"Yep. Too dang easy. I know I should, but..."

"Ah-huh. I get it. I assume you didn't go after that guy before because you needed more evidence."

"You're right there, but I think I let it go on too long. Here we are. Your car will be safe enough on the street here."

"It's stolen anyway," replied Kara. She was grinning. "Took it off a drug dealer."

"You're a bad woman, Lady Blue, you know that?"

Kara giggled. "So I've heard."

They were chatting easily as they reached headquarters. "For Moragah. For Justice."

Intel was pacing as they entered. "Hey, Boss. You guys finish up that bit of business?"

"Nope," replied Tasha. "I dealt with the commissioner, but the mayor is in the wind somewhere. Probably in a safe house somewhere."

"Crap. I was hoping that was done so you could focus elsewhere."

"Why, Intel? What's up?"

"The beast is gone."

"What???"

"The men heard a small ruckus earlier. They took a peek and he is gone, vanished, nobody home at the lair."

"Oh damn, that can't be good," sighed Tasha.

"Any idea at all where he might go?" asked Intel.

"None at all."

"I think I might," said Kara.

"Care to share?" asked Tasha.

"You said he could barely speak until recently, right?"

"Yup."

"After you guys got attacked and he ate a couple of dead cops he could talk much better, right? Said his name was Dan? Where did that name come from?"

"Probably from one of the men he fed on," replied Intel. "Oh shit, you think he's gone to that man's house?"

"If that's who he thinks he is," said Kara. "That's where he's likely to go."

"I gotta call Jess," said Tasha, fishing her phone from her pocket. She thumbed it onto speaker as it was answered.

"Tasha, what the hell is the matter with you? You can't just call me like this. I'm at work, investigating the mess you made at the commissioner's house. Jesus..."

"Jess, shut the hell up and listen. The monster is gone."

"What??? What monster? What the hell..."

"Listen, I told you about him. He learns from what he eats. We believe he ate a few of those men you guys sent into the sewers the other night. He says his name is Dan."

"Why the hell should I care what his bloody name is?"

"Jess, he's gone. We think that he thinks he's the policeman named Dan. We think he's headed for that man's house. You've got to find out who that was, where he lived, and get his family away from there. This creature is dangerous."

"Shit. Got it. Thank you, anonymous tipster. We'll get right on that." "Officer Briggs, is the chief here yet?"

"Just arrived, Ma'am. He's over there."

Jessica followed the man's direction and easily found the chief. "This looks like the work of Lady Justice," he said.

"I agree, Chief." She leaned closer and spoke softly so only he could here. His eyes went wide then he whipped out his phone. Ten minutes later she was in a police car racing across town to a more modest area. She arrived to find the neighborhood in an uproar. As the two cars came to a stop the people rushed them shouting, "Monster!"

"All right, settle down, folks," said Jessica as she spoke through the bullhorn and tried to reestablish order. There were a lot of upset and frightened people. Several were waving around rifles. "Settle down. You people with firearms, put them away or face arrest." Reluctantly, the gun toting members of the crowd returned to their homes.

Jessica directed the other police officers to take statements while she interviewed the woman who owned the house. "So, you say this man..."

"Monster. It looked like Frankenstein."

"Frakenstein was the mad scientist, he built the monster. Sorry, irrelevant. Okay, so this monster, it tried to get into your house?"

"It was in my house. It tore the door off the hinges. I know this sounds crazy, but it called me by name. It said it was Dan, my husband. He's missing and presumed dead. At least that's what you people told me. Could that thing really have been my husband?"

"No ma'am, it couldn't. I'm truly sorry, but your husband is dead."

"I know you believe that officer, but..."

"Ma'am, that beast lives down in the sewers. Your husband encountered it while on a mission, his whole team did. None of them came back. I have no idea why it thinks it's your husband, or why it left the sewers. Did it harm you?"

"What? No. No, it didn't. Honestly, Officer, I screamed and then threatened it with a knife from the kitchen. It almost looked like I hurt its feelings. Actually, when it saw its own reflection in the hall mirror..." She paused, reflecting.

"What?"

"I can't be sure, but I think it started to cry. I don't think it meant to hurt me, but it did scare the hell out of me."

"I can believe that. What happened next?"

"Well, I was screaming at it to get out and it did. By then people were outside. They saw it and started screaming too. Others came running with guns, but it had run away."

"Did you see which way it went?" She pointed in the general direction of the military zone. Just then Jessica's radio squawked. There had been several sightings two blocks over. She got back in her car and headed out.

After trailing it for several blocks she was sure it was headed home. While the other officers were taking statements, she called Tasha. "I'm on the trail of Frankenstein's Monster. It's headed back your way."

"Good to know. We'll be on the lookout. Thanks, Jess. Oh, any idea where the mayor is hiding out?"

"No, but I'll poke around a bit."

"Thanks, Jess. You rock."

"And don't you forget it. Be safe, Tash."

"Well, that's it, guys," said Tasha as she dropped her phone back in her pocket. "Dan is heading home. Trouble is, he's got a lot of folks following him and a lot of them are carrying guns. God forbid they allow anything a bit different to live. Some days I hate humans."

"Easy, girl," said Kara as she took Tasha's arm. "You said yourself, Dan is dangerous. It was one thing to leave him be when he stayed in his lair, but it's something else again to have him running loose in the city. You and I need to get out there." Tasha nodded and followed her out, snatching up her flute as they went. Kara saw but made no comment.

When they reached the surface they found the soldiers clearing folks off the streets. "It's for your own safety, folks. We'll sound the all-clear once the danger has passed." They paused and reached out with their distance hearing.

"That way," said Tasha as she set out. She'd caught the sounds of distant gunfire and wailing sirens. With Kara at her side, she raced away on full combat mode. Three blocks later they found the beast. He was down.

Tasha ran right past him; she'd seen the men with rifles closing in. The police had not yet arrived. Before the men could react she was on them, tearing the weapons from their hands and smashing them. "What the hell is the matter with you people," she demanded as she came down off combat mode.

"Us, what the hell is the matter with you, woman," demanded one huge man. "That rifle was worth two thousand dollars."

Tasha went nose to nose with him. "Oh yeah? What's your life worth to you, moron?"

"That thing's a monster. We have to kill it," continued the man as his companions came closer.

"Why?"

"Why? Because it's a monster, that's why. We have to protect our families."

"Did it hurt you? Did it hurt a member of your family? Did it threaten you?"

"Well, no, but it's a monster, for Christ's sake."

"Only one of several here tonight," said Kara as she bent the barrel of another rifle. "He's down, Justice. You go see to him. I'll deal with this." Tasha nodded and went to the huge body lying on the ground. It was still alive.

Kara glared at the now disarmed men. "You idiots owe me your lives. That's Lady Justice. You know what she does to people who fire guns in her city?" Three of the men gulped and backed away.

At that point the police cars arrived. Officers poured out onto the street, guns at the ready. With a wave of her arm Kara created a wall of flame between Tasha and the police. She easily leaped through the fire to join her friend. They could hear the police swearing behind the wall of flames. "How is he, Tash?"

"Not good. Not good at all."

"What do you want to do?"

"Leave me here," wheezed the beast, fighting for breath. "Save yourselves."

"No."

"Yes, Lady Justice. I'm just a monster. Run while you can."

"The hell I will. Kara, help me here. Careful, his skin burns like the devil." She peeled off her Kevlar vest and used it to protect her hands as she lifted up the huge body. Kara shucked off her vest and took the other side. Together they helped him towards a manhole.

Tasha hurled the cover away then they struggled to lower him down. They made it just as the police cars came around the block. The police were instantly surrounded by heavily armed military. The girls could hear Intel talking to them. "Go back, we'll deal with this."

"Yeah, well just make sure that damn monster is dead."

"We'll deal with this. Go back. We have no desire to harm you, but you're in military territory and pushing your luck. Go back. Leave this to us." Reluctantly, the police left.

The girls were struggling along with the beast who couldn't do a lot to help himself. "Boss?"

"Intel, give Kara your vest. His skin's already burned through hers."

"Leave me. Save yourselves."

"Shut up, Dan." Tasha's jaw was clenched tightly. Her vest had burned away too and her forearms felt like they were on fire.

Intel gave Kara his vest then peeled off his jacket, wrapping it around his arm he took Tasha's place. A little further on the beast groaned. "Water. Put me in the water, there." They weren't at the lair yet, but they did as he asked. They lowered him into the sludgy waters and he disappeared under the surface.

"Think he'll make it, Boss?"

"No idea, Intel. Thanks for helping. I know what you'd rather have done."

"I had no option; I know what you women are like."

"What's that supposed to mean?" asked Kara.

"My wife was always bringing home cats. I had no choice, but I refused to clean the cat box."

"I didn't know you're married," said Tasha.

"Yeah, well, technically, she's a widow. The military reported me dead; she got the pension money and was mad as hell when I showed up at her door. So was her new boyfriend."

"Well that sucks," said Kara.

"Truly it does. Come on, ladies. You've done all you can here. Now we have to get you home and patch up those burns."

"They're healing already," replied Tasha, "but I agree. Let's go home. I'm done for the day."

When they reached headquarters Tasha fairly melted onto a bed and went to sleep. Intel was gazing at her, concerned. "She's not fully healed," said Kara, "but I couldn't hold her down any longer. She'd have been okay, but the business with the monster finished her. I'll ask Moragah to give her another healing."

Intel nodded then sighed. "I guess I'll have to requisition new uniforms and armor for you two."

"Yeah, we can be hard on gear all right."

"War's like that," he replied. "You should get some rest too."

"Count on it," she said as she sank to the floor beside Tasha and closed her eyes. "Lady Moragah."

"*I am here, Kara.*"

"Lady, Tasha could use another healing."

"*Yes, Kara. She will sleep long and awake renewed, as will you, my priestess.*"

"Thanks, Moragah. You rock."

Kara was filled with a wave of healing warmth, like a hug from the mother goddess. She smiled at the mirth in Moragah's voice. "*Sleep well, my daughter.*"

A Short Breather

K ara awakened alone, Intel and Finder working at their maps quietly. "Morning, boys. What's new?"

"Not a lot," replied Finder. "Your new uniforms and armor should arrive in a couple of days. The news is full of last night's exploits and the TV folks are all over Miss Murdock for another interview with Lady Justice."

"Speaking of Tasha, any idea where she might be?"

"She's down at the lair. Just follow the sound of the flute."

"Thanks, Finder. First things first." She headed for the washroom at the platform then returned and followed Tasha to the beast's lair. She could hear the soft, soulful melody coming from up ahead. It sounded like someone was in mourning.

As Kara stepped through the opening to the lair, the labored voice of the beast spoke. "I see you, Lady Blue."

"I see you too, Dan. How are you doing?"

"I'm healing, slowly." Tasha stopped playing. The beast's voice sounded so sad. "I'm not Dan."

"I know," said Tasha.

"I thought I was Dan. Why did I think that?"

"You learn from what you eat."

"Ah, he must have been one of those who came here and shot me."

"That was our guess too," replied Kara. "So, you're going to make it?"

"Yes. That's a problem for you and your friends, Lady Justice."

"What do you mean?"

"If I stay here, one day you will have to kill me. You don't want to do that, I know."

"It doesn't have to be that way."

"Yes," he replied, "it does. You know it's true. You asked if there are others like me. There are. I can feel them, but I don't know where they are, just far away.

"Once I heal, I will leave here. I will seek them out, wherever they are."

Kara sighed and lowered herself to the floor beside Tasha. "Look, big fella, humans are everywhere. You already know what they're like."

"Yes, Lady Blue, I know. They will hunt me as they hunt you."

"Then why go?" asked Tasha.

"You saved my life. I don't know why, but I won't have my fate in your hands, friend Justice. No, I will seek the others. That way my fate will be in my own hands. Good bye, friends." With that he sank beneath the surface of the waters.

Tasha leaped to her feet, but Kara caught her arm and stopped her. They felt his presence fade as he moved away from them, deeper into the sewers to heal, and then to move on. "Let him go, Tash. Let him go. You did all you could, now it's his turn to explore the world, to make a life for himself."

Tasha turned and buried her face in Kara's shoulder. She allowed herself one long sob then stopped and stood back. "Sorry, Kara, sorry. I know what that does to you, I..."

"Hush, it's okay, come back here." She pulled Tasha back onto her shoulder and let the distraught girl sob her heart out.

Eventually Tasha stopped sobbing and pulled back again. "Kara, I..."

"It's okay, my sister in Moragah. It's okay. That was way more about your mom and dad than about Dan, wasn't it?"

"Yeah, it was. I just never got the chance to mourn them. I know what happened to you, I know why you don't like to be touched, and I wouldn't..."

"Stop now," said Kara, a gentle smile on her elfin features. She pulled Tasha close again and hugged her gently. "It's okay." Tasha returned the hug, a single sob escaping her again. "We lead solitary lives, Tash. We have to, so it's okay to steal a hug or a shoulder to cry on when we're together."

Suddenly the vast presence of Moragah enveloped them like a mother's arms. "*Kara is correct, Tasha. In ages past, the priestesses had to be strong for the people, and in private, for each other. Be at peace, my daughters.*"

"Moragah, what will happen to Dan?"

"*I don't know, Tasha. However, I will tell you this, you have changed him. The anger and rage inside him have receded somewhat. You brought him peace of the spirit through your music. You taught him compassion through your selfless acts on his behalf. I do not know what fate awaits him, but he has withdrawn from the darkness of spirit. He may yet find a place in this world.*"

"Then I'm okay with it all, I guess. Thank you Moragah."

"*Be blessed, my children.*" With that there was a gentle wave of healing energy then She withdrew.

"You okay now, Tash?"

"I am. Kara, thanks for that, and for everything."

Kara gave her arm a gentle squeeze. A sudden bright smile lit up her face. "Come on, woman, I'm hungry. Let's go see if we can scare up a meal at the mission."

They returned to headquarters and informed Intel Dan was gone. "Gone? As in not coming back?"

"That's what he said, Intel," replied Tasha. "He said he was going looking for the others like him."

"Not so sure that's a good thing."

"Who knows, but at least I was able to save a life instead of taking one. I didn't have to kill an innocent."

"Yeah, I guess you're right, Boss. So, we can reclaim that section of the passages?"

"Yup. You guys do that. Kara and I are headed for the mission for some grub."

"Casey's Cafe has better grub and less praying," grinned Decoy as he handed them a wad of cash. "We had a visit from a street gang last night. They're buying."

"Works for me," said Kara as she took the money and passed it to Tasha. "Let's go before I waste away." Laughing, Tasha followed her out.

"I'd say something happened down in those tunnels this morning," mused Intel as he watched them walk away.

"Whatever it was, it wasn't a bad thing," said Decoy. "Lady J hasn't looked that good for quite a while."

"Second that. Okay, let's go check out the lair and make doubly sure the beast has gone."

Alicia Murdock found them at the cafe. "Hi kids, mind if I join you for a coffee?"

"Join away," smiled Kara.

She sat and took a sip of her coffee, her eyes twinkling with mischief. "You're pretty bold, sitting with the likes of us," said Tasha.

"Me bold? How about the two of you sitting here in broad daylight."

"Yeah, well, the zone is the only place we can do that," replied Tasha. "It actually feels good. So, how's the job going?"

"Awesome. Tasha, I can't tell you how good it feels to be the real me, doing what I always wanted to do."

"Tell us, what's newsworthy these days?" asked Kara.

"Well, let's see. Lady Justice finally caught up with the commissioner. I covered that story. Then I had to go monster hunting, interviewed a number of terrified people, and a number of wackos who claim Lady Justice and Lady Blue were working with the monster to terrorize the city. That was interesting."

"I'll just bet," grinned Tasha. "How's Bill liking his new job?"

"He's actually enjoying it, J. I haven't seen him this good since Momma died. Somebody else is missing you, though."

"Missing me? Looking for my head, is more likely. I stood her up last night to go hunting."

"Ah, she's the forgiving type, you'll be fine."

"Ah-huh. You could do a lot worse, Alli." Tasha grinned wickedly.

"Huh? What are you talking about?"

"You know damn well what I'm talking about. You and Jess. You're a natural."

"Except I'm not natural."

"Oh shut up," sighed Kara. "If the woman is worth a grain of salt, that won't matter. And if it does, she's not worthy of you. So stow the pity party, grow a pair of boobs, and make a move. Stop being a fraidy puss."

Alicia grinned and blushed at the same time. "That's what I love about you most, Kara, your gentle diplomatic ways. Can we change the subject now?"

"I wondered when you'd get down to business," said Tasha. "What's on your mind, Allie?"

"I want to do another interview with Lady Justice. Wait now, hear me out. The mayor has gone to ground, and I can't find a trace of him. I'm getting blocked at every turn, but I do know who has him."

"Oh? Do tell," said Tasha.

"The feds have him hidden away in the city someplace. They're also looking for you."

"They can get in line," sighed Tasha. "Okay, so how is an interview going to help?"

"You've got the goods on him. Not everything was leaked to the public when he was charged. Poke him with something new and maybe he'll stick his head out long enough to deny it. He's a politician, after all. They always deny everything on camera."

"Okay, it's worth a shot. You got a cameraman you can trust?"

"Amy could do it. She's good with a camera. You'll have to pry her loose from Intel, but you're tough, you can do it."

Tasha chuckled. "Yeah, he's taken quite a shine to her all right. Okay, I have just the spot. We'll do it down in the lair."

An hour later they were in the lair. Tasha was in her war gear with full battle makeup on. Alicia stood in front of the camera. "Good evening, ladies and gentlemen. This is Alicia Murdock coming to you from deep in the bowels of the city. A place called the lair. We were brought here blindfolded to meet with Lady Justice. She's supposed to meet us but... She's right behind me, isn't she?"

She turned to see Tasha standing in the shadows behind her. Tasha stepped forward. "Lady Justice, thank you for agreeing to this interview..."

"My message is for the mayor of this city," said Lady Justice, her voice sounding deep and harsh. Her eyes were ablaze with barely controlled fury as she stepped forward. "Mr. Mayor, a few weeks ago you declared war on me. You sent dozens of police forces against me. They're all dead now. Are you happy? Are we done with this yet?

"How many more police will die trying to hide your crimes. I have evidence of your involvement in polluting this city with toxic waste. I have evidence of your involvement in a rape gang during college, and I have evidence of your involvement in the murder of my parents. For these and many other crimes, you will face justice." She stepped closer to the camera, looking sinister. "I'm coming for you, rapist, murderer." At that she stepped back against the wall and disappeared.

Amy lowered the camera. "Where did she go?"

"Who knows. Now we wait for a guide to get us out of here." With that she shut off the recorder. Tasha reappeared and led them back to headquarters.

IN AN OLDER HOUSE IN a more rundown part of town, the mayor faced his angry wife and daughter. "Rape gang, Wilton? What the hell is she talking about?"

"That's a lie, Ellen. I categorically deny every word of those specious accusations. I..."

"Oh shut up." He had never seen his wife so angry. "She says she has evidence. I believe her. That young woman who approached us at the protest rally last Spring was right, wasn't she? She is your daughter, isn't she?"

"No. No, listen. It's all a bunch of lies meant to discredit me. I'm going to call a news conference for noon tomorrow. I'll set the record straight."

"That's a seriously bad idea," said a hard eyed man in a cheap suit. "She's trying to flush you out. You'll be wide open and hard as hell to protect."

"Look, this killer strikes from hiding, at night," replied the mayor. "She's no sniper. I'll be back here long before dark, safe and sound."

"I really don't like this, not one bit. The deal was we keep you safe, but you remain in hiding until the trial. What the hell is the problem anyway? Your political career is over, why do you care?"

"Because I do, that's why." The mayor was angry now. He pulled out his phone and dialed. He didn't dare say, but this was his only chance to save his family. If he could cast enough doubt on what Lady Justice had said he could bluff his way through the rest. If he could cause enough doubt his jealous wife would settle down.

As he finished arranging the press conference for the front steps of City Hall, he found his daughter facing him. "What? Don't tell me you believe these lies too?"

"Is it true, Daddy? Do I really have a sister?"

"No you do not. I don't want to hear any more about this foolishness."

"Did you order that woman's parents killed?"

"No, now be quiet, Jill. I will not be cross examined by my own family." They all spent the rest of the evening in bitter silence. The federal agent spent his time arranging security for the press conference.

At the appointed time the mayor arrived at City Hall and faced the cameras. Alicia was there, jostling with the rest for a chance to get in a question. It was business as usual. The mayor stood at the podium, his lawyer at his side, and made his indignant speech, denied everything, and called for a renewed war on Lady Justice. He finished and headed back to the waiting limo, carefully guarded by the police who also fended off the press.

The limo took a circuitous route back to the safe house without incident. As they all settled down with a drink, the agent spoke. "That was too damned easy. I don't like it."

"You have good instincts," said a soft voice. Tasha, in full war paint, stepped away from the wall. He went for his gun, but she was instantly on him, stripping the weapon away and knocking him back onto the sofa beside the mayor's wife and daughter. His own gun was pointing at him. "Toss it away."

"What? You've got my gun. Toss what away?"

"Your spare. Nobody else move or I start shooting."

"There are more guards outside," said the daughter.

"No there aren't," replied Tasha. There was a soft code knock at the door. "Come in, Blue." A small woman in battle fatigues entered. She had blue spirals on her face and forehead. She didn't speak, just caught the gun Tasha tossed to her.

"Now, Mr. Mayor..." He leaped to his feet and tried to run. He didn't get far. He was spun around and thrown to the floor face down. Tasha hauled him to his feet as the women both screamed. Her powerful arms encircled his neck.

"As I was saying, for the rape of Danita Kells, the attempted murder of your daughter, Monicia Kells, and for the ordered murder of my parents..."

"Wait, please wait." That was the daughter. "Please don't kill my father."

"He killed mine."

"No, he didn't. He couldn't have, please."

The wife sighed deeply. "She's right, you know. He didn't order your parents killed."

Tasha still held the man in her grip. A quick twist of her arms and his neck would be broken. She paused and looked closely at the two women. The daughter was clearly frightened, distraught, pleading for her father's life. The wife was not. "Convince me."

"Mamma?"

"You're the killer who calls herself Lady Justice, right?" said Ellen. "Well, here's the god's honest truth, Justice. This man is a sniveling coward. He would never have the courage to order anyone killed. As long as I've known him he has been an obedient lap dog to his college buddy, the former commissioner. If it was indeed you who killed that one, you did the world a favor. Harlan was scum and would have no problem at all giving that order.

"On the subject of the rape, if they did rape that woman as you say, then it is indeed his daughter whom she bore. Harlan was unable to create a child. His wife tried for years. As soon as she left him she started popping them out like rabbits.

"On the subject of the pollution, I'm sure you're right about that. So what's it to be, Lady Justice? Revenge or justice? Yes, he's a sniveling rapist, I've no doubt, but does that carry the death sentence?"

"You should have been the mayor," said Tasha. She dropped the man in her arms. "According to the law he's as guilty of murder as the commissioner was, but I'm not the law. Still, there needs to be some justice here, if not for me, then for Monica Kells."

She turned to the federal agent. "Tell me, why are the fed protecting this guy?"

"He worked a deal," replied the man. "He's got the goods on a lot of seriously bad people."

"So he'll testify in exchange for immunity, right? After all he's done he walks away free as a bird, and I spend the rest of my life on the run?"

"Yeah," replied the agent, not meeting her eyes. "That about covers it."

"Well, that seriously sucks," said Tasha, a cold deadly note creeping into her voice. "There has to be some justice here.

"All right, Mr. Mayor, you owe your life to your wife. You can work that out when I'm gone. First, here's what you're going to do. You're going to resign as mayor first thing tomorrow. You are also going to publicly acknowledge Monica Kells as your daughter. Do this and I'm clear, you'll never see me again. Fail me and you pay the price."

She faced the wife. "I'm trusting you to see he follows through."

"That's the price of my life?"

"Not yours, his."

The daughter was now holding her father. "Wait, please."

"What is it?" asked Tasha.

"You're convinced this Kells woman is my sister?"

"If I wasn't sure I wouldn't have said. I've seen her mother's diaries."

"Do you know how to contact these people?"

"I can reach Monica. Her mother died of cancer last year."

"Can you put me in touch with her? Please?"

"Why?"

"She's my sister. I want to get to know her."

"She's black."

"What the hell does that have to do with anything?"

"Means a lot to some people," said Tasha, still stone cold.

"Well not to me," replied Jill as she rose to her feet. "She's my sister and I want to meet her."

Tasha gazed into her eyes for a long moment then relented. "Pass me your phone." Jill hesitated for only a second then fetched her purse and passed over the phone. Tasha thumbed it on then dialed. She put it on speaker.

"Hello?"

"Monica, it's Justice."

"Hey there. Good to hear from you. What's up?"

"There's somebody here who wants to talk to you. Says she's your sister."

Tasha passed over the phone and Jill took it eagerly. "Hello, Monica? I'm Jill. I believe we're sisters and I want to meet you." That conversation continued, but Tasha and Blue had disappeared. The bemused agent saw his gun resting in the wife's hands, but he hadn't seen Tasha hand it over. He grabbed it and leaped to his feet. The two other agents outside were just beginning to recover consciousness. The ladies Blue and Justice were nowhere to be found.

"Feels weird, doesn't it, Tash?" asked Kara as she drove back towards the military zone.

"Huh?"

"When it's over," replied Kara. "It feels weird when you finally put the last piece of the puzzle in place and deal with it."

"Yeah, it does, actually. I feel almost empty. I thought I'd feel something when I finally closed the door on the case of my parents' killers. I thought there would be a bit of sweetness there, but nothing. I guess Moragah is right. Revenge is a hollow prize at best. Knowing I've put a lot of bully boys out of action with this feels better. She knew it would."

Kara giggled. "Well, She is a goddess after all."

Tasha laughed with her, and the tension eased from her body. "Turn there."

"Okay. Where are we going?"

"Graveyard. I want to tell Mom and Dad it's over. I got the guys who killed them, and I exposed the bad guys Dad was trying to stop. They can rest now. It's finished and I'm okay."

Kara nodded but didn't speak. She parked at the gate and followed Tasha inside. Kara held back a few paces as Tasha sank to a cross-legged position between the graves of her parents. She listened quietly as Tasha told them of her adventures and successes. As Tasha pulled out her flute and began to play softly, Kara felt another presence beside her.

"You'd be Lady Blue," the woman in police uniform said.

"That's me. You Jessica Logan?"

"Yes. When I heard of your visit to the mayor I knew I'd find her here. Is she going to be all right, Lady Blue?"

"Kara. Yeah, she is, Jess."

"I wish I could be as certain about that."

"You can."

"How?"

Kara smiled. "I'll tell you a secret. I'm going to stop running around all over the country looking for trouble. It's time I settled down."

"You're staying here?"

"Yup. Jess, Tasha goes so cold on the hunt and when the action starts. It's almost like she has no feeling at all, good or bad. I think she needs a touch of humanity around to keep her honest."

"And to watch her back?"

"Damn right."

Jessica sighed deeply and nodded. "Then I'm okay. Kara, thank you."

"For?"

"Being there when she needed it, for doing what I couldn't even if I'd been there."

"Still love the girl, don't you?"

"Always will, but that's okay. We can't ever be together, and we both know it. Please take care of her."

"I will, I promise."

"Thank you, Lady Blue. It was a pleasure to meet you."

"You too, Jess. Take care."

Jessica smiled and walked away. Kara turned back to listen as Tasha continued to play. "Is that okay, Moragah, if I stay?"

"*I was going to suggest it, Kara. You are correct. She will need you.*"

Kara smiled as Moragah drew back and Tasha arose, replacing the flute in her belt. "Come on, Blue," she smiled. "Take me home."

The End

AUTHOR: AND NOW FOR a peek at the next book in the Children of the Goddess series.

Lady Shadow

by

Prudence MacLeod

Mistake

Everyone makes mistakes. Even a goddess can make a mistake. Giving things a second thought, Moragah wondered if she gave Lady Justice too much power. Secretly, Moragah gave a little push to help Justice remain human. She hoped it would be enough, as a frightened voice in a distant city called out to be heard.

Stupid Mistake

C urled up in her favorite chair, dressed in her PJs, Lexa Condon sighed with contentment. Lovingly, she opened her book and dove into the world of adventure, leaving the stress filled world, and the past due rent, behind. Hours later she slowly withdrew her attention from the pages. Loud, shouting voices from the next apartment penetrated her awareness.

The Browns were such a quiet couple, she had never heard them raise their voices. Frowning, Lexa pressed her ear to the wall. "Goddammit, Bill, keep your voice down," shouted a male voice.

"Keep my voice down? For Christ's sake, Frank, this is our own government doing this."

"I know. So what?"

"So what? You know? How long have you known?"

"I've always known. You're such a naive fool, Bill."

"Well, we have to do something, tell somebody."

"No, we don't." There was a soft popping sound, a woman screamed, another popping sound, and then silence.

Not sure what had happened, Lexa did something completely stupid. She went next door and knocked softly. "Hey folks, is everybody all right in there?"

The door flew open, her arm was seized, and she was yanked into the room. "Hey, what the hell?" she demanded as the door was shut behind her. A man she had never seen before raised a gun with a silencer on it. He shot her. Blood spurted from her head and the world vanished as she fell to the floor.

Pain and confusion entered Lexa's awareness first as she began to regain consciousness. Her vision was blurry, but after a quick groping search she found her glasses. Settling them on her face she was suddenly confronted by the horror of her situation. She was in an apartment with two dead bodies. Lexa struggled to her feet, made it to the door then opened it a crack. The hallway was empty. She quickly slipped out and closed the door behind her.

A few swift steps found her back inside her own apartment with the door locked. Only then did she raise a hand to her aching head. It came away covered in blood. The sight in her hall mirror shocked her and she nearly fainted. Her hair was matted with dried blood and there was a gash on her skull. It burned like hellfire.

Lexa tried to clean herself up, but it hurt too much and she gave up, called a cab, and went to the hospital. She told them she had fallen and hit her head on the coffee table. "That looks like a gunshot wound," said the doctor, as he gave her an injection to kill the pain. "I have to report this to the police." Lexa nodded, then closed her eyes. She didn't really care anymore; she just wanted the pain to go away.

They shaved part of her head then dressed the wound. A nurse tried to get the blood out of the rest of her hair. It took a while, but she managed it. By the time she was finished, the police had arrived. They questioned Lexa about what happened, and she told them the truth. They left her there in the hospital room and went to investigate her claim. The officers found the bodies exactly as she described and radioed in about the homicide.

A stern faced man sat alone in his hotel room, listening to a police radio. Within moments his phone rang. "There's a witness at the hospital. Lexa Condon. Get your mess cleaned up." He thumbed it off and returned to his car.

Lexa was starting to get her mind clear. She buzzed for the nurse just as a new doctor entered the room. She recognized him instantly, and he recognized her. She threw a pillow at him and rolled off the bed. It was enough of a distraction and his shot missed.

"What the hell..." The nurse who'd just entered got no further as he turned and shot her. She fell to the floor, but an orderly had seen into the room. He shouted as he tried to drag the nurse out of the line of fire. "Gun. Call security!" Without a second's hesitation the gunman threw a chair through the window and exited down the fire escape. He was gone before security could reach the scene. Lexa lay cowering under the bed, trembling in terror.

A short while later, Lexa was in a secure room with police guards posted at the door. They'd had to sedate her, but she wasn't quite asleep. She could hear the guards talking.

"What do you think, Jim?"

"This is all way over my head. I overheard the chief and the commissioner talking. Turns out those two bodies were CIA spooks. The commissioner thinks this was an in-house cleanup operation."

"And this poor gal stumbled into the middle of it. Shit. I don't care much for her chances if a professional spook is after her."

"Yeah. I just hope I'm not on shift when it happens."

Lexa covered her ears and tried to pull the blanket over her head. Curled up in the fetal position, she trembled in fear. "It's not fair," she whispered to herself. In her beloved books, the heroine would rise from the ground, hurling lightning and death at the evil ones. She would walk through them, cutting them down like a scythe through a field of grain. She would destroy them utterly, find out who had sent them, and then take out the evil behind the evil. But she was no heroine; she was Lexa, the waitress who had lost her job because she refused to have sex with the cafe owner.

Never one who believed in god, Lexa had always preferred the heroes in her books to the rituals of religion. "Okay, there are thousands of gods being worshiped every day. This prayer is for any god out there who is listening. If you're really there, prove it. Help me."

Nothing happened and she began to weep softly, her mind still fogged with the drug. It took her a moment to realize she was no longer alone in the room.

Trying to shake the cobwebs from her mind, Lexa peeked fearfully over the blanket. The room appeared to be empty, but she was aware of another presence. "Where are you?" she asked softly.

"*I am everywhere,*" replied a warm gentle voice. It seemed to be amused.

"What are you?"

"*You called for a god, did you not? I am Moragah, and I have answered your call. I did not immediately claim you as I waited to see if another more familiar to you would make that claim. They have not, so I am here. What would you have of me?*"

"Wow, those pain meds were way better than I thought. Now I'm hallucinating."

"*Perhaps we should start again. May I touch you?*"

"What? Oh, okay I guess." Suddenly Lexa was aware of that vast presence surrounding her, relieving her pain and fear, clearing her mind. "Oh, wow," she said aloud, then whispered. "Oops, sorry. Don't want to upset the guards."

"*The guards cannot hear us, nor can the man who hunts you, find you. I have taken you between worlds and time. You can speak freely here.*"

"Cool."

"*You still believe you are hallucinating.*"

"Oh yeah, this is so cool. I can see everything even without my glasses."

Lexa felt the mirth in the voice as she was bathed in warm loving feelings. "*All right, Lexa. Let's work with that. Tell me why you called.*"

"But you already know. You said there was a man hunting me, so you know what happened."

"*Oh yes, but what I truly do not know is why you called. Even though you don't believe in gods, you called out. Why? What do you want a god to do for you?*"

"Protect me."

"*Truly, is that all you want?*"

"Well..."

"*You do not trust.*" The warmth and love Lexa felt from this vast being had her floating in bliss. She had no fear and no other desire except to be there. "*You understand that for every action there is a equal reaction. You fear what I might want in return. Very well, perhaps it will be better if I go first. Lexa, there is a darkness falling over this country, this world. The forces of darkness grow stronger in spite of efforts to oppose them. The killings of your neighbors is just one example.*

"*I want you to fight the darkness. I want you to search out those who control and direct the minions of darkness.*"

"Me? Oh no, I'm just a girl, and not a very brave one at that."

"*I know. I know you would rather hide away, but I ask you, what would the heroines of your stories do?*"

"Ha, they'd fight for you. Why don't you create one of them to be your hunter."

"*That's the idea. That's why I answered your call. If you choose to take on this task for me I will give you the tools to accomplish the task.*"

"Seriously? You'd give me superpowers? You're the best hallucination ever, Moragah. Which powers would you give me?"

"*You would have the instincts of a wild animal. You would know when danger approached, or when your prey was near. You would be stronger than ten men. When threatened or in great need you would be able to move so fast that the human eye could not follow, and this speed will enhance your strength. You would be able to hear at great distance by focusing on whatever you wanted to hear. Your injuries would heal almost immediately. These are the basics that all my priestesses have.*

"Above that, each priestess has certain abilities that are her own. Penny is absolutely tireless and can move about a city like a bird of prey. Kara controls fire, creates and controls it with her mind. Tasha can hide in plain sight, appearing and disappearing at will. Get the idea?"

"Okay, so what would be my special talent?"

"Hmm, Lexa, you have a powerful and vivid imagination. For you, I think the power of illusion."

"You mean like a magician?"

"That and much more. By focusing your will on an individual or group, they would see only what you wanted them to see, to hear only what you wished them to hear."

"So, I could make a guy think I was the most beautiful woman in the world?"

"If that was your wish, yes."

"Okay, now I know there's a catch," sighed Lexa, still basking in the glow of Moragah's loving energy.

"Ah yes, the catch. When I create a priestess I am forever a part of her, always within her and her awareness, sharing experiences with her. I try to guide her and protect her, but the life of a priestess is a life of danger. Not all survive it. Also, each day at sunrise the priestess greets me with a short blessing. Watch now and I will show you. This first one is Penny."

Lexa felt Moragah's pride in the tall blonde as she watched the girl race across the rooftops of a city. She gasped at the long falls and tumbles the fierce looking warrior took. She gulped as the woman tore into a group of armed men and took them down with ease. Next she saw the woman stand beside another and call a greeting to Moragah as they faced the rising sun.

The next was a small girl and Moragah showed a mother's pride as the diminutive warrior raced at a street gang war. Lexa gasped as the girl threw a wall of flames into the battle zone then ran into it. She reappeared moments later carrying an injured child in her arms.

She walked through the fire, but it didn't burn her. Later she greeted Moragah at sunrise just as the taller blonde had done.

"*The first was Penny,*" said Moragah. "*The second was Kara. Now for Tasha.*"

Lexa saw a dark skinned girl step out of the shadows. She was exquisitely beautiful, but her eyes were cold, so cold. She stepped out of a wall, seized a man with a gun, broke his neck and let the body fall. "Justice is served," she said as she disappeared back into the wall. Later she appeared before some sort of altar, surrounded by soldiers. "For Moragah, for Justice."

"Wow," said Lexa. "They're amazing. You want me to be like them? I could never be like them, could I?"

"*Yes, you can. That's what I want for you, Lexa. Each deals with injustice in their own way wherever they find it. For you it would be different. You would be searching for the ones who direct the injustice, the chaos of darkness. Like Penny and Kara you would battle whatever crossed your path, but like Tasha, you would be always searching, pulling the weeds of the human garden.*"

"She looked so cold, like she had no feelings at all."

"*Tasha has feelings, Lexa, but when the time of battle is on her she goes cold so she can do what must be done. It would be the same for you.*"

"Do you really think I could be like them?"

"*Yes, but it will be difficult for you at first. I would prefer to have one of them guide until you're comfortable with your new abilities. However, this will not be possible. So, what will it be, Lexa? Will you join me on the great quest, the grand adventure, or will I put you back where I found you?*"

"Okay, sure, I'll do it. Make me a super hero."

"*You still do not believe,*" said Moragah, a hint of mirth in her voice. "*You soon will. Brace yourself, this part is extremely painful, but only lasts a second. Ready?*"

"Ready," was the dreamy reply.

"*You're not, but it has to happen. Lexa, I am deeply sorry for this.*"

Suddenly every cell in her body felt like it had burst into hellfire. A soul searing scream burst from her lips and the illusion of a dream was gone. Even as the two guards burst into the room with guns drawn, Lexa felt Moragah healing and soothing her wounds. Lexa sat up in the bed, gasping and trying to regain control. "Whoa, fellas, easy. Nightmare. Bad dream. Bad drugs. Sorry."

A nurse had also hurried to the room. "I'm so sorry," she said. "Sometimes the drugs can induce nightmares. Easy now, breathe deeply. I'll call the doctor and get a different prescription for you."

"No, don't bother," replied Lexa. "That stuff just makes my brain foggy. Got anything to read? That usually calms my nerves."

"I'll get you something," said the nurse, as she hurried away. The two guards had satisfied themselves that all was well and returned to their station outside the door.

"Holy smokes. That wasn't an hallucination; it was real. You're real, Moragah."

"*Yes, my skeptical priestess.*"

"And I really have super powers?"

"*You do. The ones we discussed and a few more for you to discover on your own.*"

"Okay, so how can I test them?"

"*Pinch the bed frame.*"

She did and the metal buckled under her touch. "Wow. Okay, I'm going to need some practice before I get too crazy. So, what do I do now?"

"*Whatever you want to do, Lexa. The task is in your hands now.*"

"I think I'll stay right here and play along for a while. They may send somcone else after me. I could catch them and learn something useful from them, couldn't I?"

"*Yes, that is a sound plan.*"

"Then that's what I'll do." At that point the nurse returned with a romance novel for her. Lexa thanked her then dove into the story.

The next morning a perplexed doctor released Lexa from hospital. Her scalp wound was completely healed and the hair was already starting to grow back. She would have a scar, but once the hair grew in no one would ever see it. She had refused protective custody, so a policeman drove her home and promised they would keep an eye on her.

Lexa noticed the bloody handprint on the door and inside the apartment on the wall. That was going to be hard to clean off. She started to cry when she finally saw her reflection in the mirror. There was a scar on her scalp and the hair had been shaved at an odd angle. Drying her tears she found a scarf and tied it around her head, hiding the hair and restoring her sense of self. Suddenly she remembered. She hurried to the window and raised her arms high. "Lady Moragah, I'm so sorry. The sun is up, and I forgot. Wait, a blessing. Hmmm, Moragah, I thank you for this new day to enjoy and for saving my life. May your name ever be revered and blessed." She lowered her arms and turned away. *"I hope that was okay,"* she thought.

"That was wonderful, Lexa, my daughter." Moragah engulfed her in warm loving energy like a mother's hug. Lexa sighed with contentment and relaxed. "So, do you have a plan for today, my priestess?"

"Today, Lady, I plan to make a plan. You've given me life and powers that only happen in books. I need to learn what they are and how to use them. I also need to keep a sharp eye out. That man will come for me again; I know he will. That's why I came home, so he'd come for me in a place where I feel familiar. Darn it, I wish I was rich and had a fancy surveillance system."

"Do you need such a thing?"

"It wouldn't hurt." Lexa felt Moragah's mirth and she, too, smiled. "Okay, what have I missed?"

"What would your favorite heroine do?"

"Easy. She'd meditate and see everything around her with her eyes closed. Wait, are you saying I can do that, too?" For an answer, Moragah just gave her another wave of warm loving energy then withdrew to let her work. "Great," Lexa sighed aloud. "She gave me a fancy bicycle, but no training wheels. Okay, let's give it a try."

She sank to a cross-legged position on the floor and closed her eyes. She took a few deep breaths, then tried to picture the hallway outside her door. The image flickered for a second, then cleared. Amazed, Lexa watched as another resident emerged and locked her door before walking to the elevator. The elevator went up instead of down.

Next she tried the stairs, although she rarely used them. She saw a young couple, teenagers, in the stairwell, kissing. She moved her awareness on to the parking garage. It was empty of people, but there was a note on the windshield of her old car. "Miss Condon, you rent is two weeks past due." Oh crap. "Wait, I could read that. There's the proof I need." Lexa leaped to her feet and ran from the apartment. She fairly danced down the stairs. "Hey, break it up, you two," she said, as she passed the kissing teens. The boy told her to fuck off. Ignoring him, she ran on. The note was on her car, just as she'd seen. "Oh my god, it's real."

"*Of course it is,*" came Moragah's amused voice.

Lexa laughed and danced around. "Oh man, this is so cool. Moragah, you rock." She took the elevator back to her floor. The door had locked behind her. "Oh crap. Now I have to go ask Mr. Jones to open the door and I don't have the rent. Dammit. Wait, maybe I don't." Lexa focused her mind on the door, picturing the locks turning from the other side of the door. She heard the click as it unlocked. Another victory dance followed as she swung the door open wide.

Lexa stopped dancing and sank gracefully to the floor again. "Now for the rent." All her attempts to magic up the rent failed, and she finally gave up. "Okay, that one's a bust. How am I going to get the darn rent? I could go out at night and unlock the doors to the bank?

No, I'm not supposed to be a burglar, I'm supposed to be a superhero. Maybe I could save somebody, and they could reward me..., no, that would be wrong too, I guess. What then? Maybe I should ask the boss. Moragah?"

"*I am here, Lexa.*" Moragah's voice clearly conveyed her amusement.

"You're having way too much fun at my expense."

"*I am truly enjoying you, Lexa. I'm quite proud of you. You're doing fine.*"

"Fine? I'm about to become homeless."

"*As was Penny in the early days, and Tasha as well.*"

"How did they survive? I mean, what did they do for money?"

"*They took it from the villains they defeated. They still do.*"

"Okay, so if I dress up a bit then go out to the bad part of town I could... No, that would be wrong. It would make me like them. I have to find somebody to rescue then I can take the money from the bully, right?"

"*You could do that.*"

"I get the impression you wouldn't approve. Me neither, really. Dang it..." At that point Lexa heard a noise at her door. She couldn't see it from where she sat, but her extra sight kicked in. It was the assassin breaking in. Lexa's eyes grew wide with terror, but she caught herself. "No, I can take this guy, and he has information I need." By this time he was inside, closing the door softly behind him.

He saw her as she rose from the floor. He raised his gun, but she thrust a hand towards him and spoke a single word in a deep, demonic voice. "Dragon!" He screamed in terror as the dark serpentine beast rose above him, great jaws opening wide, head thrusting forward as the foot-long fangs reached for his body. He emptied his gun into the ceiling then fell to the floor as the jaws of death closed on him. He did not move again.

Lexa swallowed hard and approached him carefully. She had seen the dragon, but only as an illusion. To the assassin it had been real. He had literally died of fright. Lexa checked for a pulse and found none. "Shit." She stomped her foot in frustration. "I needed information, not a body. Now what the hell am I going to do? Think, Lexa, think. Okay, check his pockets."

She emptied his pockets then took stock. There were two extra magazines for the gun, fully loaded, the gun with silencer, but she had no idea how to use it. Ah well. There was a wad of cash totaling eight hundred dollars; that she could use. Chewing gum, lighter - but no smokes, car key - a rental, and a hotel key. "Hmm, might learn something there."

Lexa grabbed the phone book and looked up the hotel's location. She nodded then grabbed her coat. She swung by the manager's suite to pay the rent with the cash she'd taken from the body, then headed for her car. She stepped into the parking area and froze. "What if he put a bomb under my car? Shit, now what am I going to do? Wait, his car. He wouldn't have put a bomb in that, and I might get some information from it. Okay, where is it?"

Heading for the guest parking spaces she held the keys up and pressed the button. There was a soft toot of a horn and a car's lights flickered. "Nice ride," she said, as she settled herself inside. She pulled out onto the street, then drove to the hotel. She parked the car then began to search it. The search turned up nothing, so she headed inside and went up to the room.

The room contained a few of the man's personal belongings. Clothes with no labels, a watch and wedding ring in the pocket of a suit jacket. Further patting down of the jacket turned up a small cell phone. It had a message on it. "Is it done?"

"No, it bloody well isn't," she muttered, as she searched the rest of his clothes. Nothing further turned up, except the soft breathing of a human being. The sounds of those careful breaths slowly penetrated

Lexa's awareness. She stepped into the bathroom and closed her eyes. There it was, a woman with a gun, hiding behind the floor length drapes. "Come out from behind those drapes if you want to survive. Toss the gun first."

For a moment nothing happened, then the gun thumped onto the floor and the woman stepped out where she could be seen. Lexa came out of the bathroom holding the empty gun with the silencer on it. "Step away from the gun and sit on the bed. Good girl, now, who are you and what are you doing here?"

"I could ask you the same question."

"Fair enough, you first."

The woman gave her a puzzled look then shrugged. "My name is Ellen Cameron. I'm a private detective. I've been hired by your boyfriend's wife to catch him in the act."

"The act of what?"

"Adultery."

"Oh. Okay, got any ID?" Slowly, carefully the woman pulled her ID out of her jacket pocket and tossed it onto the other bed near Lexa. Lexa flipped it open and inspected it for a moment then tossed the empty gun on the bed beside it. "Okay, my turn, I guess. A few days ago this guy shot and killed my neighbors. I heard something and went to look. He shot me too, but didn't finish me. He tried twice more since that, but failed both times. That's his gun, I took it off his dead body."

"Really?"

"Really."

"You must be a lot tougher than you look, kid."

"Apparently, I am. My name's Lexa Condon and I really need your help."

"My help?" Lexa nodded. "Okay, how can I help? I don't come cheap, you know. I have expenses and..."

"Wait. Hush, someone's coming." Footsteps approached the door and stopped. Lexa waved her hand, indicating the woman should step back. They heard the key in the lock and Lexa waved her hand.

The man who should have been there suddenly appeared with a naked woman in his arms. The door swept open, two shots were fired from a gun with silencer and the couple fell. The gun withdrew and the door closed tightly. Lexa let the vision of the two people fade as she sighed and sat heavily on the bed.

"Sweet Christ," breathed the detective. "How the hell did you do that? Who are you? What are you?"

"I already told you; my name's Lexa and I'm scared to death. Can we get out of here and talk some place safe. I'll tell you everything and explain how we can help each other."

The detective scooped up her gun. "Good idea, let's go." Lexa started to follow her to the door. "That got your fingerprints on it?" She was pointing to the gun with silencer on the bed. Lexa nodded. "Better bring it for now. Keep it out of sight."

They rode down the elevator then walked out to the parking lot. "You got a car?"

"Just the guy's rental," replied Lexa. "It's over there. I took it because I was afraid he might have put a bomb in mine."

"Okay. Leave it for now, but we'll have to get your prints out of there too. For now we'll take mine." She led Lexa to a small but fast-looking car and they got inside. Ellen started the engine and pulled out into traffic. She went to a drive through and bought coffee for them both then parked the car. "All right, I'm listening," she said, as she passed one coffee to Lexa.

Don't miss out!

Visit the website below and you can sign up to receive emails whenever Prudence MacLeod publishes a new book. There's no charge and no obligation.

https://books2read.com/r/B-A-ZKBBB-BIMTC

Also by Prudence MacLeod

Children of the Goddess
Lady Blue
Fallen Angel
Lady Justice

Forgotten Worlds
Suvi
Echo of the Past
Survivors
Ship
Fleet
Unite
IGEN
T.E.N.

Nova series
Novan Witch
Assassin of Nova
Beyond Nova
Claimstake

Red Nova

Watch for more at https://www.prudencemacleod.com/.

Telling a story is like knitting a sweater. Start with a ball of possibilities, pull out one small thread and begin. With luck and patience you will create something quite wonderful.

About the Author

On a far off windswept island Jennifer Crandall sits with her dogs and cats creating fantastic stories for all to enjoy. She publishes as JL Crandall, Prudence MacLeod, and Jenni Leigh.

Read more at https://www.prudencemacleod.com/.

www.ingramcontent.com/pod-product-compliance
Lightning Source LLC
Chambersburg PA
CBHW030256200626
46816CB00002BA/671